Alien Bootlegger

Conversation Pieces

A Small Paperback Series from Aqueduct Press

Subscriptions available: www.aqueductpress.com

Fall 2004

Spring 2005

Fall 2005

About the Aqueduct Press Conversation Pieces Series

The feminist engaged with sf is passionately interested in challenging the way things are, passionately determined to understand how everything works. It is my constant sense of our feminist-sf present as a grand conversation that enables me to trace its existence into the past and from there see its trajectory extending into our future. A genealogy for feminist sf would not constitute a chart depicting direct lineages but would offer us an ever-shifting, fluid mosaic, the individual tiles of which we will probably only ever partially access. What could be more in the spirit of feminist sf than to conceptualize a genealogy that explicitly manifests our own communities across not only space but also time?

Aqueduct's small paperback series, Conversation Pieces, aims to both document and facilitate the "grand conversation." The Conversation Pieces series presents a wide variety of texts, including short fiction (which may not always be sf and may not necessarily even be feminist), essays, speeches, manifestoes, poetry, interviews, correspondence, and group discussions. Many of the texts are reprinted material, but some are new. The grand conversation reaches at least as far back as Mary Shelley and extends, in our speculations and visions, into the continually-created future. In Jonathan Goldberg's words, "To look forward to the history that will be, one must look at and retell the history that has been told." And that is what Conversation Pieces is all about.

L. Timmel Duchamp

Jonathan Goldberg, "The History That Will Be" in Louise Fradenburg and Carla Freccero, eds., *Premodern Sexualities* (New York and London: Routledge, 1996)

Books by Rebecca Ore

Series

Becoming Alien

Becoming Alien (1988)

Being Alien (1988)

Human to Human (1990)

Novels

The Illegal Rebirth of Billy the Kid (1991)

Slow Funeral (1994)

Gaia's Toys (1995)

Outlaw School (2000)

Collections

Alien Bootlegger and Other Stories (1993)

Conversation Pieces
Volume 9

Alien Bootlegger

Novella

by

Rebecca Ore

Published by Aqueduct Press
PO Box 95787
Seattle, WA 98145-2787
www.aqueductpress.com

Cover Design by Lynne Jensen Lampe
Book Design by Kathryn Wilham
Original Block Print of Mary Shelley by Justin Kempton:
www.writersmugs.com

Cover photo of Pleiades Star Cluster
NASA Hubble Telescope Images, STScI-2004-20
http://hubble.nasa.gov/image-gallery/astronomy-images.html
Credit: NASA, ESA, and AURA/Caltech

Printed in the USA

Introduction

Every writer worth admiring has her place of power, that locale or perspective from which she does her best and most assured work. For Rebecca Ore, it's the Blue Ridge Mountains of southwestern Virginia. Though she has lived much of her life elsewhere, the land and its people are in her bones and the rhythm of their speech lodged in her head. It's not an easy place to love, and she returns to it always with a certain degree of pain and regret. But it's the forge and wellspring of *Alien Bootlegger*

The Blue Ridge area is a region of stunning beauty where guns are common, old wealth holds to traditional values ("like owning people," as Rebecca enjoys explaining), and operating an illegal still is not so much disreputable as a matter of cultural pride. It's not like the North, where I grew up, but it sure isn't the South people tell you about either. It doesn't parse out like other places. It's its own thing.

Nobody has ever written so well about or with such insight into this corner of the world as Rebecca does. She presents it without condescension or sentimentality. She knows the social networks and how they connect. She's got the speech down pat. Mostly, though, she knows how the people think. I've lived in the area, and I'm here to tell you that a "foreigner" (as they call outsiders) can hear some good stories and experience some strange times there—but he's never going to get to know the truth of their lives, the core stuff, the meat. Only someone who belongs has access to that.

Yet, though Rebecca's family has had strong associations with Patrick County dating back to 1812, she grew up in Clemson, South Carolina, and Louisville, Kentucky. And though she always read science fiction and was a writer from an early age, her original metier was not SF but poetry. It was a long and twisty road that brought her to this genre.

Here's the short version: By age 19, Rebecca had been published in *Red Clay Reader*. A year later, she ran off to New York City to become a poet. She found a job. She led *la vie boheme*. She published poetry and had a mimeographed book or two. She worked for a year for the Science Fiction Book Club. She attended Columbia University School of General Studies. She became a reporter for *The Enterprise* in Patrick County (that's one county over from Franklin), where she got to know the sorts of people—state's attorneys, chicken-fighters, sheriffs—that poets don't. She went to grad school at SUNY-Albany. She moved to Critz, Virginia. She taught at a business college. A friend (me) wrote her, saying, "Rebecca, you've got to get out of Critz!" She moved to Philadelphia. She got involved in computers. Today she teaches at both Temple and Drexel. With a career path like that, it's hardly any surprise that Rebecca has a quirky and independent perspective on pretty much everything.

And somewhere in there, after Albany but well before Philadelphia, she became an acclaimed science fiction writer.

So why, out of all the places she's been and lived, does Rebecca choose to write about Franklin County? Because of the deep loam of family stories and connections, to be sure. But also because, as she explained to me once, this is where human beings are to be found in their natural habitat. Not domesticated humans, mind you. Not law-respecting city dwellers whose lives and emotions are under their careful control, but folks who have never entirely bought their way into civilization. Wild humans.

Wild humans live on their own, off at the edge of society, rather like urban raccoons. Everyone knows they don't belong—not to anything or anybody but themselves. They have messy lives driven by furious emotions, and the law only holds as much authority over them as they choose to give it. Wild humans are often outcasts, and inevitably outlaws.

This is a story about them. Which is to say, this is a story about us.

—Michael Swanwick

Alien Bootlegger

1

Lilly Nelson at the Hardware Store

When I first saw the alien was the first warm day after a terrible winter of layoffs. Years like these, men stare at the seed packs, the catalogues for fertilizer spreaders, and wonder if they've got enough land for a distiller's corn crop. Or would the mills hire back soon enough as to make farming superfluous? Rocky Mount was full that day of men speculating about turning back to what their ancestors did back when southwestern Virginia was the frontier. Sort of like what didn't starve out the great-grandparents won't starve out us. But few had kept their tractors. No one had draft animals. The ancestors had hated farming like crazy, and the descendents really wanted the factories to start hiring again. But, meantime, let's get some equipment clerk to distract us or go out and gossip about the alien.

My own business wasn't off—none of my DUI clients had written me a bad check yet—but I'd still gone to the hardware store, even knowing how crowded it would be. I needed my own distraction. Fibroids waited in my uterus for a sonogram on Tuesday, so today, I hefted plastic mesh bags full of spring bulbs, comparing the lies on the package flap to the real flowers I'd seen the last summer I'd planted them.

Just my luck, I'd have to have surgery. Odd, I'd never wanted children, and it would have been absurd to have a child to take care of when I was forty-three and had my aunt Berenice to worry about, but to have it come to this. Then while I was drinking a Dr. Pepper for the caffeine to soothe my addiction headache and waiting for a clerk to sell me some dahlias, the alien walked in and I was finally distracted.

Nobody wanted to act like a gawking hick. We watched each other to time one quick stare apiece, aiming our eyes when nobody else was looking. The hardware store itself looked weird after I looked away. The alien jolted my eyes into seeing more detail than I'd ever noticed before—dead flies on a fly strip, the little bumps in the plastic weave under my fingers, a cracked front tooth in the clerk's face as he came around the counter.

"Welding equipment," the alien said as a nervous man in a business suit tugged on one of his long bony arms. "Stainless-steel welding equipment, stainless-steel pipe, stainless sheets, stainless-steel milk tank."

The clerk looked at me, I nodded, meaning *okay, deal with that first.*

As the clerk came to him, the alien adjusted the flow on an acetylene torch. He looked like a man crossed with a preying mantis, something a farmer watched for crop-damaging tendencies. In the chitinous head, the eyes looked more jelly-like than decent, though I suspect my own eyes in that head would look just as bad. Actually, the eyes were more or less like human eyes; it was the ears that were faceted like stereo speakers. Big enough. Little indentations inside the facets. I bet it could tell you precisely where a noise was coming from.

So, here the alien is, one of the ones about which we've been reading all the reassurances the government chose to give us, I thought. One was hiking the Japanese central mountain crest trail. That was the one the media went crazy over, but others were living in Africa working on tilapia and other food-fish recombinant DNA projects and weaving handicrafts or in Europe taking sailing lessons or studying automotive mechanics. They'd all arrived in an FTL ship and said they were tourists. Yeah, sure, but they had that FTL ship and we didn't.

"Lilly, told you I been seeing saucers since 1990 down in Wytheville off I-77 junction," a bootlegger's driver said to me. I looked at the man and wondered if he was driving for one of the DeSpain cousins now. Berenice always was curious about the DeSpains, as though they were a natural phenomenon, not criminals at all. She accused me of resenting criminals who made more money than I did.

"Look at its ears," I said, meaning *lets not talk until it's out of the building at least.*

He considered them and looked back at me with tighter lips.

I shrugged and visualized the fibroids down inside me, flattened sea cucumbers, squirming around. Maybe the alien would bring us better medicine? He bought his equipment and said, "Pickup truck with diplomatic plates."

"Bring it around to the side," the clerk said, trying to sound normal, almost making it.

After the alien left, the bootlegger's driver said, "What is he planning to weld stainless for?"

We all knew one of the options—still-making, no lead salts in stainless-steel boys' product, and the metal was cheaper than copper. Or maybe he was setting up a dairy? "Maybe he's a romantic." I paused. "You ever consider working for Coors?" I said before walking back to the office. I knew his answer before he could have replied—driving legal was a boring ass job; driving illegal was an adventure.

Tomorrow was Legal Aid; so I wanted to get the partnership papers filed on the Witherspoon Craft Factory before five. I dreaded Legal Aid. When times were bad, the men screamed at their wives and children, and the women wanted divorces. If he beats you, I'd always say, I'll help you, but just for yelling at you, come on, honey, you can't support kids on seven dollars an hour. Better to dust off the old copper pot and get a gristmill, clean the coil, fill a propane tank, and cook some local color in the basement that tax evaders and tourists pay good money for.

When we heard the aliens were just tourists, the first joke everyone in Franklin County seemed to have heard or simultaneously invented was if having one around was going to drive up real estate taxes again.

When I got into the office, the answering machine was blinking. My aunt Berenice spoke off the disc: "I remembered hearing where Patty Hurst was hiding, but I think it was just some fire-mouthing. Even then, I was getting too old for simple rhetoric. Bring me something… I forget now…when you come home. And, Lilly, your message makes you sound impossibly country."

It wasn't that she was that senile, Berenice was simply righteously paranoid from a long radical life. I made a note to pick up some single scotch malt from Bobby. He was making fine liquor for now. An independent, but maybe everyone would leave him alone because he made such classic liquor. And he had hospital bills to pay. Pre-existing condition in his child.

Then I wondered why I wasn't more excited about the alien. Maybe because I had so much to worry about myself, like who was going to take care of Berenice when I went under the knife?

I filed the partnership papers at the courthouse and drove by Bobby's to pick up the single malt. When I pulled up at his house, he was sitting on the porch, twitching a straw in his hand.

"Bobby," I said. He had to know what I was here for.

"Yo, Luce. I had a visitor today."

"Um," meaning *are you going to be a client of mine any time soon?*

"One of the DeSpains."

"You been aging it for five years. . ."

He interrupted, "More."

"So, didn't you just slip it to friends like I suggested? It's not like you do it for a living."

"I do need the money. But I wanted to make really good liquor. Seemed less desperate that way."

"It's fine liquor," I said.

"It was fine liquor," Bobby said. "DeSpain isn't going to make me his man."

"Well, Bobby," I said, watching the straw still rolling between his hands, "be careful." What could I tell him? Dennis DeSpain wasn't the roughest cousin, and nothing in the liquor business was as rough as the drug business. "You don't have any liquor now?" Bobby shook his head, the straw pausing a second. Now I had to stop by the ABC store before I went home. Daddy always said legal liquor had artificial dyes and synthetic odors in it.

When I got up to go, Bobby said, "I guess my wife will have to start waiting tables over at the Lake. I'm just lucky I'm on first shift. In the dye house." We both knew why the dye house never laid anyone off—the heat drove close to one hundred percent turnovers there.

"When I was younger," I said as I got my car keys back out of my purse, "I was going to reform the world. Then, Franklin County. Now…"

"Yeah, now," Bobby said.

"Well, I won't have you as a client, then."

He jerked his shoulders. "I don't know what I thought I was doing."

"Liquor-making the old way is a fine craft."

"Oh, shut the fuck up, Lilly. I thought if I did it fine, it wouldn't be so desperate. Man with bad debts turns to making liquor."

So, bad times and no simple solutions. I sighed and got in the car, then remembered the alien buying stainless-steel welding equipment, his fingers longer than a man's but fiddling with the valve with the same bent-head attention as a skilled human.

I drove back to the ABC store. The alien was leaning against the wall of the ABC store, eating Fig Newtons. At his feet was an ABC store brown bag full of what looked like sampler bottles. The man with him looked even more nervous than when I'd seen the two of them in the hardware store, furtive like. When the alien opened his mouth to bite, I saw his teeth were either crusted with tartar or very weird. They were also rounded, like a child draws teeth, not squared. He stopped to watch me go in. When I came out with the legal malt whiskey, I nodded to him.

"Lawyer," he said. "Ex-radical. Wanted to meet you, but not so much by accident that you'd be suspicious." I went zero to the bone. The voice seemed synthetic, the intonation off even though the accent was utter broadcast journalism.

"He's very interested in Franklin County," his human guide said. "And liquor." Poor guy sounded like he knew precisely why the alien had bought all the stainless-steel welding equipment and the liquor samples.

"Really?" I said, not quite asking, remembering quite well the year when most of the distillers went to stainless steel—thank God, no more of the car radiator stills that killed drinkers.

The man said, "I'm Henry Allen, with the State Department. He's Turkemaw, of Svarti, a guest of our government."

"And a vegetarian," I said, having recovered enough to pass by them and get back in my car. A farmer would try Sevrin dust or even an illegal brew of DDT if he saw the alien in a stand of corn.

I don't know why I think farmer—I've never farmed day one in my life, and I lived in New York for years. Berenice complains I sound like I'm trying to pass for redneck, but the sound's inside my head, too. Back at home, a chill intensifying with the dark, Berenice and a young black woman were sitting on the porch talking. They didn't have the porch light on, so I knew they'd been sitting there awhile, Berenice in the swing, the black woman stiff on the teak bench, both so absorbed in each other they were oblivious to the cold and dark. I tried to remember her name, Mary…no…Marie, a chemical engineering student who'd grow up to be one of those black women who'd gone to college and become plant chemical control officers, rather ferocious about her rise up. Berenice loved anyone who had ears to listen and hadn't heard all her stories yet.

As I got out of the car, I felt a bit ashamed of myself for thinking that. She'd told me enough about Marie that I should have realized Berenice listened to her, too.

When Berenice said, "And the Howe women I knew from Boston said that Emily Dickinson was a senator's daughter and that she tried like a motherfucker to get published," the girl threw her head back and laughed. Laughed without holding back, genuinely fond of my aunt, genuinely amused, so I thought better of her.

Marie said, "They don't teach me that at Tech."

"No, professors all want to believe they're more than schoolteachers, but they don't know what real poets are like." Berenice could be fierce about this. One of her husbands or lovers wrote poetry books that sold in the forties of thousands. "Always remember you're more than a chemical engineering student, Marie. Everyone is always more than the labels other people want to put on them."

"Of course, I am more than a chemical engineer," Marie said, tightening the dignity muscles again. I reminded myself of what I'd been like at eighteen and felt more compassionate to us all.

"Terrella—" Berenice began. I remembered hearing about Terrella, the black woman bootlegger in the forties who killed a man.

"Terrella," Marie said. "That kind of kin threatens me."

I set the bottle down by Berenice. She sniffed and opened it, sniffed again. "Argh, fake esters. What happened to Bobby's?"

"DeSpain."

Marie stiffened. Yeah, I remembered too late that I'd named a lover she'd just broken with. Berenice heard quite a bit about it, as Berenice, when she was in her best mind, could get people to talk. I'd hear more later. Berenice said, "Lilly, get three glasses."

"I don't want to talk about Terrella," Marie said again. As I got the little glasses we used for straight liquor, I wondered if two denials made a positive. Terrella wore long black skirts way into the fifties, with a pistol and a knife hidden in the folds. Her hair had grown into dreadlocks before we ever knew the style was a style and had a name. She left $25,000 and a house to her daughter when she died, which was remarkable for a black woman in those days, however she got the money. Berenice admired people who could work around the system and not lose, even when they were criminals. To Berenice, one should never resign oneself to any status other people thought appropriate.

"So, you're kin to Terrella," I said, putting all the glasses on the table that went with the bench and pouring us each about an inch of the Scotch.

"I'm even kin to Hugous, the man who runs The Door 18."

"Smart man," Berenice said. "Terrella was smart, too."

"She was a hoodlum," Marie said. "Hugous—"

"Hugous puts money aside, no matter how he makes it," Berenice said. "That's always useful in a capitalist state. Considering that sloppy capitalism's all we have to work with." Berenice freed her long grey hair to dangle radical-hippie style and grinned at me. So, she'd always been looser and more tolerant than I. I had enough rigidity to get a law degree so I could support her. Retirement homes, even ones better than she could have afforded, terrified her.

Not that we weren't more two of a kind than anyone else in the county, but I always wanted to organize the poor while she thought the poor ought to kick liberal ass as well as boss ass.

"I saw the alien today after I made the appointment for the sonogram," I said.

"Fibroids. Mother had them," Berenice said. "They thought they were cancer and sent her womb to Wake Forest."

"Jesus, Berenice," Marie said. "That's like hearing Dennis talk about jail rape."

So, I wondered, what was the context? Did Dennis rape or get raped? Berenice picked up her scotch and drank it all down in one swallow, the crepey skin jerking on her scrawny neck, the long grey hair flying. "So, Marie, you like your life?"

"It's fine," the girl said tonelessly. "I like Montgomery County better than here."

Meaning gossip in Rocky Mount about Dennis De-Spain was a problem, I thought, and none of the Tech students knew yet that she had outlaw kin. I looked at Berenice. Marie got up to go, her hyper correct suit wrinkled anyway around her rump. I watched as she got in her little Honda.

"Berenice, I saw the alien buying welding equipment."

Berenice said in a conspiratorial whisper, "Marie can weld, too."

"DeSpain won't like that."

"Dennis taught Marie about bootlegging. She left him because he tempted her."

"Tempted her? I mean, it isn't like half of Rocky Mount didn't see them having breakfast and smelling of come last fall."

"Tempted her to become a bootlegger. I suspect it's become like any other supervisory job to Dennis, and he needs to have someone new see him as glamorous and dangerous."

"Jesus, I thought he was half-about in the Klan, certainly able to fuck blacks, but not able to admit they've got brains as good as a white boy's."

"Marie's definitely smarter than most white boys." Berenice looked for the clip she'd pulled out of her hair and tucked all her hair in the clip behind her neck again. "She's specializing in alcohols and esters. State's going to legalize liquor-making one of these days to get some of the taxes."

"Why would a Tech student want to make liquor?" I said, angry that she'd risk a college degree for something that trivial. Not so trivial, perhaps, if one were Bobby sweating in a polyester dye house for two dollars an hour over minimum wage, but for a chemical engineering student—stupid.

"I didn't say she was making liquor now," Berenice said. She looked down at her hands, then rubbed a large brown patch between her index finger knuckle and her thumb. "First sign I had I was getting old were wrinkles going up and down my fingers on the palm side. Nobody ever warned me about them. I like Marie, but the youth doesn't rub off, does it?"

"Berenice, there's an alien in Franklin County."

"So, the government put it here. We never have any real say, do we? Alien? No different than a foreigner in most folks' minds." *Foreigner* means from outside our home county. The Welsh brought the concept with them, which is only fitting as *welsh* means foreigner in Anglo-Saxon. Berenice continued, "You think Marie's sad, don't you? Like self-cultural genocide? Maybe she'd be happier if she were more like Terrella?"

"Cultural genocide is a stupid term. It trivializes things like really murdered people."

"Well, then I'll just say she's awful divided against herself then."

"Are we supposed to judge blacks?

"It's racist not to," Berenice said, and I realized she'd been teasing me. Berenice could be such a yoyo, but she'd ceased to take herself seriously without giving up what had been good about her ideals. Taking her in, I had to watch her mind wobble, but right now, Berenice seemed fine, not bitterly ironic, not lapsing into the past because the present jammed in short-term memory, three-minute chunks throwing each past three minutes into oblivion. "Lilly, you're sure you're going to have to have surgery?" She asked sharply as though needing surgery was my fault.

If I did have cancer, Berenice would be extremely pissed. She'd have to go to a nursing home. The jittery insistence I tolerated for the delight she was on good days would get drugged out of her. I nodded, then said yes, because she wasn't looking at me directly.

Berenice poured herself another whiskey, drained it, and said, "I've lived fully, interestingly. I'd rather lose my present than my past. At least, senility won't suck that away. Did I tell you about the time I hitchhiked down to Big Sur and met Henry Miller?"

Not that she hadn't had senile moments already, I thought in pity. Then I realized I had not heard about Henry Miller and said, "Tell me."

DeSpain in Tailwater

DeSpain cast out with his Orvis rod, the Hardy Princess reel waiting for a big brown trout to inhale his Martin's Crook rigged behind the gold-plated spinner. He was missing Marie, wanted her back, and wanted to kill her, but he'd do a sixteen-inch-plus trout instead.

Or, break the law and kill a little one. But DeSpain had principles. He broke the law only for serious money. One of his nephews who'd gone to Johns Hopkins said that DeSpain was trying to work sympathetic magic with the law.

The Smith River fell with the sun as the Danville and Martinsville offices and factories turned out their lights. *All but poachers out of the water in half an hour.* DeSpain remembered what the guide told him about tying on a stonefly nymph, but he hated strike indicators and fishing something he couldn't see upstream.

Intending this to be the last cast of the day, DeSpain pulled up the sink tip and cast the big wet fly and the spinner across the river, shooting out line, then reeling in. Then he saw the alien, standing in bare legs in the cold Smith River, casting with the guide, coming on the opposite bank. DeSpain realized that the alien was two feet longer in the legs than the guide, who was up to his hips in the river, closer to the bank than the alien.

DeSpain yelled, "I knew the Smith was famous nationally, but this is ridiculous."

The alien said, "DeSpain. Liquor distributor. Still maker."

The Smith wasn't chilly enough to suit DeSpain right then, and his waders were much too warm. He'd heard the alien was rude. Correct—rude or very alien. DeSpain remembered gossip about the alien and said, "Turkemaw, Svarti resident extraterrestrial, mate went back home after two weeks here." He felt better.

"Dennis, you fishing a stonefly nymph?" the guide asked.

DeSpain pretended not to hear and left his line in the water, no orange foam strike indicator on the leader, obviously either real cocky about his skill with upwater nymphs or not fishing one.

The alien pushed a button on a small box hanging like a locket around his neck. The box laughed.

DeSpain remembered hearing last week from one of his drivers that the alien had bought stainless steel welding rods and that its farm had corn acreage. Everyone wondered if so conspicuous a creature was going to be so very more flagrantly making liquor. Or maybe the creature was making spaceships in its basement? "Be careful," he said to both of them. After they waded on, DeSpain caught the spinner and fly in his hand, then switched to the stonefly nymph.

A trout took it. As he played it, then reeled it in, it came jaws out of the water, eyeballs rolled to see the hook in its mouth. He netted it, then measured it:

fifteen inches three-quarters. *We can fix that,* DeSpain thought, as he broke the fish's spine and stretched. *Bingo, sixteen and one-tenth. The hell I work sympathetic magic with the law.*

Satisfied with the dead trout, DeSpain left the river, his eidetic memory reviewing his investments, both legal and illegal ones. *I have to be so mean with the illegal ones.* Fourteen trucks out with piggyback stills, $200,000 in an Uzbek metallurgical firm, $50,000 in Central Asian cotton mills, and maybe $500,000 in various inventories, legal and illegal.

His brain began to run more detail, like a self-programming and overeager computer. No spreadsheets, he thought as he began to wonder again if he'd bought into the global equivalent of just another Franklin County. He had first wondered if the Armenians were cheating him, but then he considered he was damn apt at bullying other men into working for him. Let other people run their butts off when the law came to blow a still.

The true reality of the world wasn't Tokyo's glitter, DeSpain had long since decided after one trip to Tokyo, but the harsh little deals driven in places like Rocky Mount and Uralsk. Tokyo and New York could evaporate. The small traders would still be off making deals, machine oil under their nails, doing the world's real business.

But that nigger bitch got away from him like no man had ever been able to. Goddamn great body and smart, too. He had a lust like a pain for women like her and his wife Orris. Yeah, Orris, she only wanted him to have simple women on the side.

He pulled the rod apart and wound down the line to keep the two sections together and the fly hook in the keeper. The trunk security chimed as he opened it. He pushed the code buttons and put the rod and vest in it before he stripped off his waders and boots and put them in a bag, then laid the trout carefully on ice, making sure it stayed stretched out.

Remembering that he paid four hundred dollars to get a ten percent casting improvement over the cheaper generic rod, DeSpain thought, *Wouldn't do that in business, but. . .*

"If you want to just kill trout, may I suggest a spinning rod," the clerk had said in tones that condemned meat fishing and people too cheap or insensitive to the nuances of a four hundred dollar rod.

Liquor. A man needs the illegal to bankroll him for the legal. "It's not romantic with me," he said out loud, thinking about the folklorist who'd come from Ferrum to tape his father about his grandfather's suicide after the feds broke his ring in the thirties.

DeSpain felt a touch of guilt that he was sending bootleg money out of the country, but no more than when he yanked an extra fraction inch out of a Smith River brown so that it would go over sixteen inches. He turned the key in the Volvo's ignition and drove home.

His wife came out when she heard the garage door open. When she wore her red silk dress like she was, she expected to go out to eat. Her hair was blowing, but instead of reaching to smooth it, she folded her arms across her breasts. DeSpain pulled on into the garage and turned off the electric eye. "Orris," DeSpain said in the garage, "what did you fix for dinner?"

"Steven's at Mother's. You owe me, Dennis. The bitch is a college student. You've even taken her out for breakfast."

"Why does that make it different? She's just another one of my dancing girl friends. I'm tired."

"I can drive myself to Roanoke if you're that tired. I know what it means when a man wants to talk to a woman in the morning. And you were telling her about still workings. At breakfast."

DeSpain knew if he stayed home Orris would harangue his ass off about that bitch, Marie. When a particular black woman was seducing him out of moonshine technology and college tuition, then he should have known Orris would see the woman as a real rival. "Okay, let's go. You don't have to drive." He wouldn't tell her that Marie had left him.

"To the Japanese place."

The Japanese place made Dennis nervous. Orris had picked up more about Japan than he had. "I need to log some items on the bulletin board." He watched Orris carefully for a loosening of those arms before he went inside. He got his Toshiba out of the safe, unfolded, it and plugged in the phone line. His bat file brought up all his bulletin boards: Posse Commitatus, the Junk Market, Technology Today, and Loose Trade. He pushed for the Loose Trade bulletin board and scanned through the messages. All his messages were coded:

TO RICHARD CROOK: BOONE MILLS LOST HUBCAP, FOUND, NO PROBLEM. GOT GAS AT THE USUAL. SPINNER.

TO MR. MAX: COLLEAGUES REALLY APPRECI-
ATED THE LOBSTER. WOULD LIKE TO ORDER
DOZEN MORE CHICKEN-SIZED.

TO RICHARD CROOK: HOPE CAN BUY ANOTH-
ER FIVE LAMB'S FLEECES, WASHABLE TANNED.

TO BUD G.R. HARESEAR: NEED SOME SENSE
OF PROGRESS REPORT.

One of his trucks had almost been busted at the
Cave Spring I-81 exit Exxon station. Three of his sup-
pliers needed deliveries. DeSpain made code notes and
purged the messages. Then he noticed that the alien
was asking in plain text if anyone wanted to sell it an
old tractor. *Why is he on this bulletin board?* DeSpain swore
he'd bring in the feds if the alien was going to be able
to distill openly when people had to be discreet about
it. *Fool, the feds brought the alien here to begin with.*

After DeSpain exited Loose Trade, he took his ac-
counting discs out of his safe. He needed to ship out
twenty-seven gallons to the small bars and then collect
on some of the larger accounts. Follett's salary came
due again. DeSpain paid his men full rate when they
were in jail and half rate when they were on probation and not working a full schedule, but Follett would
be off probation next week. Damn Follett, DeSpain
thought, he just sits there when he's raided. Most of
his still men had never been busted. He wrote a check
on his hardware store account.

An image of the researcher listening to his grand-
mother came to mind, all romantic-ass about the business and believing the guff that no one ever died at a
still raid, that both sides of the game had an understanding. Yeah, and the mountain counties averaged a
murder a week in the twenties and thirties.

His grandfather wouldn't have hanged himself over a game.

Orris came in and said, as though she hadn't been bitching at him minutes earlier, "I hope your foreign investments do well."

DeSpain rubbed his eyes and said, "I've got to go back over there in September."

"I'd like to go with you this time."

"Babe, it's just like Detroit over there. Really."

"If you went to Detroit for a month, I'd want to come along."

He wasn't sure if she were implying anything further, so he decided to just stomp change the subject. "You think I should wear a suit?" Wrong, that sounded hick asking his more sophisticated wife what to wear in the larger sense. DeSpain learned how to dress at Emory & Henry before they threw him out for getting arrested.

She said, "It's not Sunday."

"Man who looks like he was just in the river they know is rich enough not to care what a waiter thinks. Mud equals real estate."

Orris said, "Not on a nigger or a neck, mud doesn't."

DeSpain wondered if she thought her red dress would look like polyester if he didn't dress to match. He said, "I'll change," and she stepped her skinny body out on her high heels without indicating whether she was pleased on not. *Orris, an Iris root.* DeSpain had looked it up once and wondered who in her family knew such an arcane thing.

He folded his computer and put all his records and it back in the safe, then found a blue suit to wear with a string tie. String ties made Orris nervous.

On the drive to Roanoke, she said, "Don't do that to me again."

"What, with a college student?" Dennis realized she knew the affair was over, but did she know the how and why?

"Right, Dennis."

"And if I did it with some poor-ass good old girl, I'd probably be fucking your family."

"So crude, but then what was I to expect, marrying a bootlegger."

"Not that I'm not employing half your cousins. The bitch left me, if that's any damn consolation."

She laughed, then said, "One of my friends said at least recently you'd been more considerate."

Stomp change again. "Did I tell you I saw the alien when I was fishing?"

"Dennis, you are so obvious when you don't want to talk about something. I heard he was rich."

"I suppose. He had a guide with him."

"And I've heard he's rude. Is he?"

"He told me to my face I was a still maker and a liquor investor."

"Maybe he's just alien, doesn't know not to think out loud. At least, he didn't tell you how he knew about Marie."

"Gee, Orris, you can find the good side of anyone, can't you?"

"Not everyone," Orris said. They pulled up to the restaurant and walked in. "I need sashimi tonight," she said as if eating raw fish took guts.

MARIE

Sometimes I play black and tough, but not at Tech. It'd be too easy to slide from a Dennis DeSpain to a drunk rich frat boy who knows his daddy's lawyer will get him off if he leaves a woman to strangle in ropes, or to a cracker trucker with a knife.

I hate my colorful ancestors, the liquor queens, the Jesus priestesses. Times were I suspected they just re-named a Dahomey god Jesus so they could keep on writhing to him.

But here I was, home for the weekend in a brick house in a compound that reminded me unpleasantly of anthropology class, the whole lineage spread kraal-style from broke-down trailers to $100,000 brick ranch houses with $20,000 in landscaping.

We were at least in one of the nice houses; Momma was waiting for me. "You broke with DeSpain like I told you. I'm satisfied."

"Yes, ma'm."

"I saw what you were taking at Tech when your grades came. We're not paying for you to learn bootlegging."

"Chemical engineering, Mamma."

She sat down on the piano bench and closed her eyes. I sat down on one of the red velvet armchairs and leaned my head back against the antimacassar. "I know they can use you at DuPont or in a dye house. Find a place that will pay you to take a Masters in Business. Daddy's been knowing a white boy all his life that's now doing that."

21

I wondered if we'd moved away from the trailer kin what my life would have been like. I could have grown up in Charlotte, North Carolina—black, white, and mulatto all doing airy things like architecture and graphic design. Momma saw the look on my face and said, "Do you think you collected all the white blood in the family?"

"No, Mamma."

"You white granddaddies better than that DeSpain."

Lapsing out of Proper English again, Mamma? I rolled my eyes at her and said, "I need be studying." Yeah, yeah, I know Black English grammar has its own formality and I was hashing it.

"You need the computer?"

"Maybe I shouldn't have come home for the weekend. It's so depressing around here."

"You are an example to your kin."

I thought about Granny crocheting billions of antimacassars like giant mutant snowflakes, rabidly industrious while her sisters slid by on their asses. "Do you think they really appreciate it?"

Momma asked, half interested and half to abruptly change the subject, "Is there really an alien down near Endicott?"

"He was walking around Rocky Mount, trying to pass for a good old boy. Yeah, let me get on the computer." Momma grew up associating computers with school as they didn't have node numbers and nets and gossip by the megabyte when she was coming along. I could access all sorts of trash while she thought I was studying.

Orris had left me a message on Loose Trade: DEN-NIS'S DANCING GIRLFRIEND: SORRY, BETTER

LUCK/CHOICE NEXT TIME. I felt my tongue begin to throb; I'd pushed against my teeth so hard.

But before I sniped back at her, I noticed messages about the alien: ALIEN IS A BASTARD. HEARD WHEN PEOPLE CLAIM THEY WERE KIDNAPPED BY HIM, HE SAYS HE DOESN'T REMEMBER THEM IN A WAY THAT MAKES EVEN CRAZY PEOPLE FEEL REAL TRIVIAL.

I wondered if he had really kidnapped people, if his people had.

Another message about the alien: HE'S OFF BACK ABOUT A MILE AND A HALF FROM THE HARD-TOP. WON'T LET THE HIGHWAY DEPARTMENT SELL HIM THE SURFACE TREATMENT EITHER.

I left a message to Dennis: MRS. DESPAIN CALLED. TERRELLA IF YOU WANT TO THINK OF ME THAT WAY. I knew he wanted me to be more like her than I could ever wish to be.

Then the alien came on the board in real time: PLEASE, I HOPE TO DO BUSINESS HERE. MY WIFE LEFT ME. I WISH ONLY TO LIVE QUIETLY. YOUR RESIDENT ALIEN.

Someone quickly typed back: ARE YOU FOR REAL?

I DON'T REMEMBER KIDNAPPING ANYONE FROM THIS COUNTY.

I wondered why an alien would be doing business on a semi-honest bulletin board and remembered Lilly saw him buying welding equipment. I typed, THIS BULLETIN BOARD ISN'T AS SECURE AS THE SYSTEMS OPERATOR MAY HAVE TOLD YOU WHEN YOU SIGNED ON.

The alien replied: IF I NEEDED SECURITY, I WOULDN'T BE ON THIS PLANET.

2

Lilly: As Alien as it Gets

The next Saturday, as I helped Berenice with her bath, I told her how startled I'd been when the alien told me my name and occupation.

"Lilly, you afraid of the alien?" she asked me, sitting in the tub covered with bubbles. I turned on the sprayer and began rinsing her hair.

"I was startled."

"Do you hate being startled at your age? I hate limping."

"Well, if you'd let me help you with the bath yesterday, you…" Nope, I needed to help her in and out of the tub all the time.

Berenice bent forward and pulled the drain lever down. "The alien wants to see you. He called here."

"Why?"

"He's on that bulletin board everyone uses for selling liquor."

"Everyone doesn't use it for selling liquor."

"DeSpain's on it. Bobby's on it." She leaned on me as she stood up, all baggy skin over what seemed to have been fairly decent muscles. I rinsed her free of soap and wrapped a towel around her. "I said I was your aunt and that I'd like to talk to him even if you couldn't come. I faxed him my Freedom of Information file."

"Does he have a name?"

"He's calling himself Turk. Can we go over this afternoon? He said it would be acceptable. You don't have any appointments."

I shrugged and walked her into her bedroom. She sat down on the bed to dry off while I got together her panties, bra, slacks, socks, and top. L.L. Bean shipped just this week the thirtieth or so pair of a shoe she'd been wearing for over five decades. She watched me pull the paper out of the toes. "I don't wear them out often these days," she said as she wiggled into the slacks and top. I put the socks on her feet, smoothing them, then slipped the shoes on, tying the knots tightly so the laces wouldn't come undone and trip her. "So, I've lived to see an alien in Franklin County."

And Berenice was going to make the most of it even if he wasn't the sort of client I wanted. I held her elbow as we walked to the car.

"Why did you fax him your Freedom of Information file?" I asked while the car ran diagnostics on the pollution control devices.

"Well, I thought an alien who came to Franklin County might be weird." She didn't want to see him unless he found the file unobjectionable.

I don't tell people about my past, but Berenice lets any one she meets know what a bit part player she was in the events of '68. And I'm being cynical because bit player is all I've been, too. But Berenice refuses to admit that anyone has more than a bit part. I said, "I hope Turk was impressed."

The car diagnostics showed that the catalytic converter would need to be replaced soon. Thanks to the reprogramming I'd done to prolong the active-with-warning phase, that probably meant the converter was gone completely by now as I'd been getting a REPLACE SOON reading for about four months.

"There is a reason to keep the car burning clean."

"I guess, Berenice," I said as I pulled out of our driveway, "but I've got to replace the air conditioner at the office first."

"Your lungs aren't as fragile as mine."

"Don't play Earth Firster with me this afternoon, okay."

"No, that's not appropriate, considering who we're going to see."

I asked, "And where does this Turk live?"

"Shooting Creek section. Patrick and Franklin. On the line. He's renting from Delacourt heirs."

I could visualize the place, three miles of mud roads, oil pan gashing rocks, then the house, some three-story family place slowly twisting to the ground, riddled with powderpost beetles. The grandchildren would own and neglect it and rent it to summer people. Or aliens, why not? Maybe the Turk liked leaking roofs?

We drove down to Ferrum and took the road toward Shooting Creek. The road was exactly as I'd imagined it, but the house looked like several military freight helicopters had to have dropped it in last week. It was a replica of a ranch house. No, just because an alien lived there didn't mean it wasn't actually a ranch house.

Berenice looked a long while, then said, "I wonder if he got the design from TV real estate channels."

The alien came up to us, his machine laughing for him. "Ladies, lawyer, radical social worker. Berenice's file fascinates."

"Where did you get the house?" I asked.

Turk said, "Restored it."

Berenice looked slightly disappointed. I tried to remember what I could about the Delacourt family, but they were as mixed a bunch as anyone in the area, from jewel thieves to corporate executives.

We followed Turk around to the kitchen entrance. The backyard looked freshly bulldozed, raw soil faintly hazed with grass seedlings. I heard an exhaust fan running and couldn't make out where the sound was, exactly. Exhaust fans in strange places trigger my sniffing reflex—but no mash odor here, or alcohol smell either.

Turk moved a few magazines—one in some alien script that could have been just another Earth language—and we sat down.

"Do you want to meet people or do you prefer to be left alone?" I asked.

His ear facets glinted as he shifted his head. "Some people," he answered. His tongue flicked out, bristled at the tip. Like a lory, I thought, a nectar-feeding parrot. He asked, "Would you like a drink?" That was the most complete sentence I'd heard him speak.

"Yes," Berenice said quickly.

The alien made the kitchen look bizarre. His hands made the brushed nickel sink fixtures look like space craft gizmos that would regulate fuel mixes or the temperature of water, just as he was doing here, filling a glass teakettle that looked like laboratory equipment.

27

The light mix—I thought—he's got weird spectrum tubes in the fixtures. Then my mind redid some parameters, and the kitchen looked like a kitchen with an alien in it, setting a glass tea kettle on a burner. Berenice tightened the muscles around her mouth. She didn't consider tea a drink.

"Why did you come to Franklin County?" I asked.

"I heard about Franklin County from time-aged analogues," Turk said as he reached up in his cupboard for glasses and a teacup. Berenice watched the teacup as though hoping it wasn't for her. "But isn't here Franklin County?" He stuck his hand back into the cupboard and came back with a bottled and bonded vodka. Berenice smiled, but sat down when her legs began to quiver.

The Turk poured vodka, then tonic into two glasses for us, then put some dried green leaves in a strainer, balanced the strainer over his own cup, and filled it from the tea kettle. He narrowed his eyes, but his face seemed bizarre even with that expression. I realized he'd made it with eyelids alone, without shifting a face muscle. His face skin was too rigid for muscles gestures to penetrate.

I moved to take the drink the Turk offered me and realized I was stiff. He came closer to Berenice with hers, recognizing her feebleness, perhaps.

It was alcohol but wasn't vodka. Berenice said, "I understand you're on Loose Trade."

An iridescent flush washed over the Turk's face. He lifted his strainer and put it in the sink. The herb he'd used in his brew wasn't tea, but wasn't anything I knew to be illegal. He added white grains, about a quarter cup, of what was either sugar or salt. A sugar or a salt,

I reminded myself, or protein crystals, not necessarily dextrose or sodium chloride.

I smelled my drink again and caught an echo of that herb smell as though he'd put a sprig of the herb in the liquor bottle.

Berenice said, "Can you drink alcohol yourself?"

"No." The alien put his tongue down close to his tea and rolled it into a tube. He dangled the fringed end in the tea for a few seconds before drawing the tea up. His eyes widened as if the tea startled him. Definitely a drug, I thought.

Berenice sipped her drink, but she kept her face carefully in neutral. She said, "You know this isn't vodka?"

"Yes," the alien said. "I would like to put Lilly on retainer." He spoke as though he'd memorized the phrase.

"I'm not a bootlegger lawyer," I said.

"Don't be so stuffy," Berenice said. "They're social outlaws."

"They all become mill owners in the end."

The alien said, "I will never become a mill owner in the end."

I stopped mentally cursing all the liquor makers and investors and looked more closely at the alien. "What is your civic standing here?"

"Resident alien," he said. "I am legally human."

"What kind of retainer?" I said, thinking about replacing the old air conditioner with one more compatible with the ozone layer.

"Ten thousand for the year. I can pay you now." He went to one of the cabinets and began laying hands on it, then pushing it. The door opened as if it were quite dense. Turk pulled out a contract and then counted out ten stacks of bills, Crestar bank wrappers still on them.

I asked, "Do you expect to get busted?"

He looked at me, flushed rainbow again, then said, "I plan to have fun."

I hated him for a second. "It's not a game for the people around here. People get killed."

"Killed is an option. Bored, not."

"Glad you feel that way. You're risking it." I looked over his contract. I'd have to defend him in any criminal or civil suit during the year of retainer for my usual fee less twenty-five percent. I sighed and signed it, then said, "You really need a checking account."

Berenice said, "Or DeSpain's broker."

Turk said, "I had most invested in a money market."

I wondered how long the aliens had been dealing with the government, and what were these aliens to an ACLU part-time radical lawyer like me. "Why me?"

The alien studied me three seconds, then said, "You're odd."

"I don't know why I'm agreeing to this."

Berenice said, "Because you get bored in Rocky Mount, too."

Turk blinked slowly at me, then nodded as if translating blinks to nods with his cross-species semiotic dictionary. I blinked at him and he triggered his laugh machine. I thought I'd gotten too old for illegal thrills, but then Berenice proved that was impossible for my lineage.

Bobby Wasn't Working

MR. B. CORN WON'T DO IT, DeSpain read on the computer screen. *Damn Bobby, I'm going to get the boys to beat him.*

He went into the bathroom and saw Orris washing her feet, rubbing them under the running tap in the tub. It reminded him of broke mountain people living in waterless shacks, hauling jugs of water up from neighbors. Her mother had grown up like that, washing bony dirty feet with water from milk cartons, in a thirty-dollar-a-month house wired for enough electricity to take care of the stove and the rented TV. Seeing Orris washing her feet made DeSpain's stomach lurch. "You need a bath, Orris, take a whole one."

"I just got my feet dirty when I was working in the garden." She looked up at him with her pale eyes. He suspected she washed her feet this way to tell him that he was only a bit further from the shacks than she.

"Bobby won't work for me."

"You do what you need to," Orris said. She got out of the way of the toilet so he could piss, which he always needed to do when he got angry. Her dress rode up her thighs as she toweled her feet dry.

"I'm glad you understand that."

"Why does washing my feet bother you so?"

"It reminds me of welfare bitches too broke to have tubs."

"I was doing it in one of our *three* tubs. You do what you need to do, Dennis, and I trust the tubs won't evaporate."

31

DeSpain thought, *don't keep leaving Steve with your mother to let him pick up hick ways, too,* but said, "I really won't trust the money until I've got a good income coming from something safe."

"Safe? Then maybe I do need to keep in practice for water conservation if you think we might end up back having to haul it from a well." Orris smiled and went out of the bathroom in her bare feet, heels chapped as though shoes were new to her.

DeSpain had kin, distant kin, living on roads so rough Social Service made visits in four-wheel-drive vehicles. "Safe. Like a marina on the lake. The Russian stuff isn't safe enough."

Orris, from her bedroom, said, "You'd be bored shitless smiling at rich foreigners and gassing their idiot two-bedroom yachts in a lake too small for an over-night cruise."

"You want one of those yachts."

"Not here. Maybe in Russia, on the Black Sea." He could tell from her voice that she was smiling.

"I guess I should call the nephews and cousins."

"Is he making liquor behind your back, Dennis?"

"He won't make it. I thought it would be great for the lake people—good liquor, fine made, aged. Run them some bull about our Scottish heritage and Bob-by's old family equipment passed on for twelve gen-erations. Look, I already do the same thing as gassing tourists' boats."

"If he quit…I don't know, Dennis. I know you can't afford to get soft-headed."

"You want to go with the boys and lay in a few licks, too?"

"Might take you up on that, Dennis."

The notion of Orris in jeans and a pillowcase hood beating a man appalled Dennis. She was strong enough, he knew. He said, "Let us men take care of it."

"Okay, Dennis, but I'll go if you need me. Maybe if I beat up his wife…"

"Well, I appreciate that, Orris." Dennis went back in his room, turned off the computer, and put the nine millimeter Beretta Orris gave him for Christmas in his briefcase. Pausing in front of the dresser, he stared at his collection of car keys and decided to take the pickup he'd gotten at the government auction. Let them take it and resell it again. He wondered if they could seize the Volvo, just because it might have come from liquor money. He pulled off his white shirt and pulled on a Japanese T-shirt he'd picked up in the Urals. Then dark glasses with the enhancer circuit in case he got caught by the dark. He grimaced at himself and added a Ford Motor Company baseball cap. Maybe some chewing tobacco? he wondered.

Orris's reflection appeared in the dresser mirror. "Wear that cap in Uralsk where nobody knows what it means," she said, "not here."

"We both hoed up our roots, haven't we?"

"It's tacky, considering what you're going out to do. Or are you stalling?"

He threw the cap on the bed and left, feeling pretty obvious in the truck that had been auctioned after seizures four times now.

His nephews and cousins were at one of their houses with a pool, barbecuing a split pig over half an oil drum full of charcoal, drinking beer, and swimming naked while their women sat around in bathing suits looking embarrassed. "Ken," DeSpain said to the cousin whose house it was, "I need a little help with Bobby." Ken had built forty houses on the lake, run drugs, and retired at thirty-four after investing in detox centers. DeSpain's broker said detox centers could lose you money if the feds stopped the Medicaid subsidy.

Ken pulled himself out of the pool and said, "Is he undercutting you?"

"No, he's just not working. Your brothers want to help me?"

"Gee, Dennis, we've got this pig on." Ken padded over to the oil drum and brushed on a mix of vinegar and red pepper, then turned the crank of the spit. He'd geared the crank so one man could roll a whole pig. "You want us to deal with it without you. Say while you're off on a lunch boat cruising the lake?"

"I'm going, too. Be nice."

"Thanks, Dennis, but I don't think so. You ought to get out of that stupid ass liquor business anyhow."

"Feds don't bother a man these days."

"Feds don't bother much since when their budgets got cut. You just do what they're not specializing in busting."

DeSpain felt like he'd gobbled down half a pound of hot pork already. "We don't have to go tonight, but I don't like someone sneaking out on me."

"You plan to beat on him, too?" Ken used a long fork to twist off some barbecue. He held the fork out to DeSpain who pinched the meat away and tasted it. "Done?" Ken asked.

"Done," DeSpain said.

"You know, we put my daughter in that Montessori school, but I made Helen go out and work to pay for it."

"Maybe I should put Steve in it, too."

"Don't know. Helen plans to have Ann go to law school, medical school, something a woman can make money on around here. Stevie, I don't know if he needs more than public school."

"Stevie will get all he needs," DeSpain said.

Ken said, "We starting to sound like women in the mommy wars. Get naked. Swim."

"I'm ready to talk to Bobby tonight." DeSpain noticed two teenaged nephews pulled up to the poolside, arms folded across the rim. "You boys want to go?"

"Beat someone up?" The one who spoke looked at the other.

DeSpain couldn't even remember their names. The family was drifting apart. But maybe tonight that was just was well. "Can we use one of the other cars?"

Ken said, "Nope. We can't afford to lose any of them."

The boys toweled off and pulled on jeans and cut off T-shirts. DeSpain grimaced. With six packs in hand, they climbed up into the truck bed.

As DeSpain drove the truck toward Bobby's, he looked up at the rearview mirror and saw the bigger nephew poke the littler one in the ribs below the shirt. They both laughed, and the little one threw up a leg as the truck turned.

Nobody's a professional anymore, DeSpain thought. He thought about taking them back to Ken's, but kept going and pulled up to Bobby's house.

Bobby came up to the door with a shotgun in his hand. "Leave me alone, DeSpain."

"Bobby, all I want is to protect you, find you good sales." DeSpain stayed in the cab of the truck.

"I won't make liquor for you."

The two nephews in the back of the truck stood up. The bigger one smiled. DeSpain looked back at them, then at Bobby and said, "I didn't come here to beat on you. But I do have a market for what you're making and can help you out with any cash-flow problems."

The bigger nephew said, "We didn't bring guns this time."

"Damn and a half," the little one said, "why didn't I bring my old AK-47? We'll have to remember that next time."

"Think a little plastique in the basement might help his attitude, Dennis," the bigger one said.

Dennis opened his briefcase and slid his hand inside, felt the Beretta, then sighed. "Bobby, I don't know what you're trying to do to me."

"I've got three shells in this, DeSpain. I can kill all you."

"Well, tonight, I guess you could, Bobby. If that's what you want to do. But I don't think it would be lawful, seeing as how I'm sitting in my truck and the boys aren't armed. You do something like that and you'll have both law and the DeSpains against you."

The boys in the back made DeSpain more nervous than Bobby himself, but they had sense enough to shut up. The little one popped open another beer. Bobby did swing the gun up slightly, DeSpain noticed. He also noticed that Bobby was trembling. When the shotgun went down again, DeSpain looked around the yard and saw a car motor dangling from a hoist, a car sitting on blocks, leads from a diagnostic computer running out one window. "Cash flow problems?" DeSpain suggested.

"Damn you, Dennis DeSpain," Bobby said.

"You don't want to kill anyone, Bobby," DeSpain said. He eased the safety off on the Beretta. Sometimes a man would shoot you when you said such a thing just to prove you wrong. Bobby's wife came out then, and he gave her the shotgun and spoke to her too softly for DeSpain to make out.

The little cousin whistled. Bobby's wife looked back as if she wanted to give the gun back to her husband, but finally went into the house.

"I hope you didn't ask her to call the sheriff, Bobby. We're here to work this out like businessmen."

"Dennis, I don't want to make liquor."

"Well, you did make the liquor, and you were looking for customers. I'm not asking you to make white liquor. That aged barley malt of yours would be real good to have around Smith Mountain Lake. Hey, Bobby, let me loan you something to get that car back together. No, let me give you something." DeSpain arched his back to get at his wallet and pulled out four hundred dollars. He stuck his arm out of the cab and said, "Won't that help?"

"You know that it would." Bobby wouldn't come take it.

Then, in the house, Bobby's sick baby cried. Bobby closed his eyes one long moment and came up and took the money. "It takes years to age. I dumped all I made, all that was aging."

"Don't worry, Bobby. We're both young men, you especially. I've got someone working accelerating the aging process. I've thought about counterfeiting bottled-in-bond liquors, to diversify, so to speak."

"Can I quit when I get out from under?" Bobby asked.

Oh, Bobby, you'll never get out from under, DeSpain thought, but he said, "Sure, Bobby. The main thing was I didn't want you calling attention to the business. Amateurs aren't often discreet enough, and if anyone gets real obvious, then the state's going to come in serious in the county."

"You made it sound like I was competing with you and you were going to beat my butt if I didn't work for you regardless."

"Well, yeah, I'd be less than honest if I said I welcomed competition, but the real concern was for the business as a whole. And you were hardly serious competition, just making fine liquor I happen to have a personal fondness for."

Bobby looked like he knew he was being lied to, but he'd settle since DeSpain fed him lies that let him keep some face. DeSpain watched him, amazed that someone could think to get into liquor-making with a face so connected to his thoughts. They both settled into an agreeable silence.

"Aw, shit, Dennis, you not going to need us to beat him up?" the bigger nephew finally said.

"Not tonight," Dennis said. "Bobby here understand my concerns. I'll take you for a treat." He drove them up to Roanoke where he called Maudie from a phone booth to see if the girl the bigger nephew liked was available.

She was. Dennis got back in the truck and drove them to the little house behind the brick fence up near Hollins—very clean women Miss Maudie had.

"Hi, Dennis, what can I do for you?" Maudie asked as she got them beyond the door. She was a skinny woman with long thick dark-blond hair, gray in it, who wore gold bangles from wristbone to elbow on her left arm, to be used as brass knuckles in a fight.

"I'll just listen to music. The boys want to have fun." Patsy, the girl his nephews thought was so neat, came out with a girl DeSpain hadn't seen before. She was a deep mountain girl, or an imitation of one, barefoot and in gingham shorts and tube top for the tourists, DeSpain thought. He grimaced at Maudie, who took his arm and led him to the parlor where a couple of high-school-looking boys sat drinking and listening to jazz piano played by a half-Black half-Chinese girl. She wore a thin blue negligee but was playing her piano so earnestly it wasn't sexy.

"She's a student at Hollins," Maudie said as she slid an iced whiskey into Dennis's hand. "She's from Mississippi."

"Aren't they all college girls?"

"Want to talk?"

Dennis sipped his drink, listening to the nephews babbling about how they'd just whipped the shit out of one of his competitors and didn't even get bloody. "No, I'm tired. Will you be needing supplies, now that I'm here?"

"Send me in more apple brandy, if you can get some. I'm tired, too. Some of these girls are absolute cunts."

"I'll let you know how the Russian deals go."

"That apartment house you told me to buy is doing reasonable, but it's too much like this to be what I'd like to do."

"What would you like to do?"

Maudie shrugged like whatever it was she was way too old and wise to try. "You know how it is, Dennis. We have to work out our own retirement plans."

The half-breed girl paused in her playing, stared at the keyboard as if pushing the keys with brain waves, then put her hands back and began playing something classical that reminded Dennis of a time he and Orris had been to the Roanoke Symphony with Orris's college roommate. He'd felt considerably uncomfortable then, but was somewhat relieved now that he could recognize the music as classical, that a half-breed whore wasn't impossibly different from him. Dennis asked Maudie, "Do you ever feel like you were leading a whole bunch of different lives, here, the other investments?

"Aren't we all?"

The half-breed girl stared at Dennis, then, playing on as if her fingers knew the keyboard better than her eyes. She sighed and looked like she was going to cry.

"Does she fuck, too?" Dennis asked.

"She's having a bad night. Let's see about someone else."

"No, I'll come back for her."

"The alien tried last night."

"Damn. He's on one of my bulletin boards, too. Just one of them in this area, isn't there?"

"Yes."

"If he's making liquor, I'm gonna collide with the bastard."

"Here here, or here on Earth?"

"Franklin County, Patrick, where ever the hell he's living now."

"Didn't say. Seemed sleazy, but I don't know how his kind's supposed to be."

"And he wanted to fuck her?" The half-breed girl's fingers jerked discords on the keyboard, and her shoulders rounded. Dennis felt sorry for her; then for an instant he wondered what Orris would say if he fucked a Hollins girl, even one in a whorehouse. "Tell the boys I didn't buy them all night," Dennis said to Maudie. He went up to the girl and put a twenty on top of the piano, then went outside to stand by his truck until the boys finished.

3

Marie Sees Something Unusual

After my spring semester exams, I took what I learned from Tech and from Dennis DeSpain and set up a mechanically cooled still. One advantage of being a black woman engineering student is that you can get your hands on such wonderful things as a twelve-volt hydro heat pump, and no one suspects you'll be making liquor with it. Run it with a transformer or solar, and your electric bill won't jump like it would running equipment with regular house current. State ABC officers and the local narcs cruise Appalachian power bills, looking for ones that are just too big.

The only house I could rent cheap enough was an old Giles County A-frame made of weird stiff foam-over-metal ribs, an early Tech architectural school folly. When I rented it, there was a big hole where a tree'd come down on it, so I had to patch it with new foam. Earlier owners and renters had done the same, so the house was mottled greys, browns, and creams, and lumpy inside and out along the corrugated foam ribs. Whatever, I liked it because it didn't look like a still house.

When I brought in the heat pump, I put it on the floor and sat in the gloom, half ironic about the thrill. Me, bootlegging.

Actually, my body missed Dennis's body. So I was reverting to Terrella with her big skirts, her dreadlocks, and her pistol, because I really wanted to call Dennis up and say, "It's okay. I don't really need you all the time."

Brain, tell the body no, I thought as I ran the heat exchanger coils into the basement water tank and then used a plumber's bit on my drill to bring them upstairs to the bedroom.

Reasonable enough to heat people with wood, but I'd cook my mash over precisely controlled electric heat.

Down under the house on the other side from the water tank, the mash, in five-gallon drums, fermented buried in compost, rigged to a meter that told me the sugar was done now. I'd used a wheat malt, since I remembered a white man friend of my grandfather's telling how wheat made the best liquor he'd run. Sprout it just a little, dry it, grind it coarse, wet it down, and add molasses and yeast, then some chicken shit. I left out the chicken shit, added nitrates and some urea instead. The mash was ready.

The still was upstairs, in the bedroom where a steady run of electricity wouldn't be suspicious. I took the heat pump and the transformer upstairs.

About halfway upstairs, I felt utterly foolish, but so? All I'd get if I were busted would be a suspended sentence. Tech wouldn't kick me out.

I opened the door to my still room and began building a marine plywood box for the cooler and coil. The wires from the coil thermocouple controlled the fan motor. I sat back on my heels wondering if I should insulate the box, then decided better to disperse heat, even with the cooking element being also thermostatically controlled. The jigsaw cut the vents for the cold air and the exhaust; then I soldered the box and fitted it around the worm.

For the cooking thermostats, I'd taken old fishtank heaters and broken the override high points, then recalibrated them so I could keep the mash around 205 degrees. The cooking pot was insulated at the sides. I went downstairs for five gallons of mash.

Rather than lift a five-gallon wooden barrel, I drained the mash into a plastic water carrier. *Don't breathe it*, I'd heard all my life. It was more vomit-provoking than peyote. I needed an activated-carbon-filter face mask. Shit, I might have to make some money on liquor to pay for all this stuff, I thought as I lugged the mash upstairs. The mash gurgled into the pot like rotten oatmeal, and I capped it quickly and began cooking.

The first couple tablespoons I threw away. That's poisonous, low-temperature fusels and esters. Then I began running the distillate into glass bottles, not quite having the equipment for another doubling still. I probed through my valved probe hole—temperature at the cap holding steady at 190 degrees, so I shouldn't be getting too much water boiling off, mostly alcohol.

Next, I'd automate, so I wouldn't have to be on site. I kept my eye on the distillate stream, and when it slowed down slightly, I ran the rest off and threw it away. Just save the middles.

As I waited for the cooker to cool, I fantasized rigging an automated still, computer-controlled, just like one of DeSpain's better operators had, hogs getting the spent mash augered up to them.

I love work with electronics and machines. I forget I'm Black and a woman, which is very restful some days.

I lifted the top and went back to town to pick up a Spraypro respirator. The clerk looked at me funny, and I realized I smelled of alcohol and mash. My hair'd frizzed half a foot beyond my head. Bad as picking up a man's odor from sex, I thought as I blushed. The clerk smiled and handed me the respirator. "Honey, I'd recommend a full-face airline respirator myself. What you got ain't good against mash fumes," he said and handed me an extra box of gas-filter canisters.

"Thanks," I said. I hate being called honey. Color-wise, molasses would be more appropriate. Now, was he going to call a distributor and report me? Fool, I told myself, you didn't show him ID.

Back at the house, I put the liquor I'd stilled off in the refrigerator and began packing the mash up in a plastic heat-seal bag, snorting through the respirator the whole time. Then I hauled the cooking vessel into the bathroom and scrubbed it out before putting the first run through. First wine, the old people called the first run.

I used an old iron to heat-seal the mash bag. I should have rigged a centrifuge to whirl out the remaining liquor. Next time, I thought as I lugged the bag downstairs, I'd find out how to process the spent mash in an ecologically correct way. Freeze-dry it and get some pigs to eat it.

The alcohol, when I doubled it, tested out at 190 proof. It tasted like straight grain alcohol, which was, after all, what it was. I wondered what chemicals made scotch scotch and not vodka. DeSpain once asked me if I could counterfeit aged liquors. I swirled the liquor in its glass jar, watching the fine fine bubbles bead up. Surely, it could be done. But this batch I poured in a small oak cask that I'd charred inside with a propane torch. I took the cask to the basement and put it in the compost bin.

Leaving the house with the bagged mash in a plastic trash can to dump in someone's field, I thought that distilling could get to be rather boring if that's all one did. Obviously, Dennis had sense enough to hire poor boys to tend still for him.

As I dumped the mash in a pig pasture, I considered I might sell the liquor at The Door 18, a juke joint near Fairystone Park, made with a real hotel door in front. Hugous, a third cousin some removed, ran it and sold liquor and marijuana to his friends. A big, even more distant kinsman played jazz bass there on weekends. I knew of the place through trailer cousins who'd taken me there a couple of times before Mamma heard about it. Back in my dorm room, I changed into something red velveteen.

It's a long drive, and I took a disc of some white guy reading a piece for next year's English as I go. The guy narrating finds someone floating in a swimming pool over a woman name Daisy when I turn off 57 to the road leading to the place. Couple miles further, there's a big dirt parking lot and two Dobermans wandering around looking for white people to bite. I sort of nod to them and push through The Door 18 and see Hugous sitting wiping glasses and smiling. The big cousin is booming out jazz chords to a hymn playing tinny from a little Taiwanese tape deck.

"Hi, Hugous, you know Albert?"

"Been knowing him since he was a baby."

"I'm his second cousin once removed. We all live on Tiggman Adams Boulevard."

"One them Crowley people."

"Yeah. You might have heard of Terrella.

"Midwife. She catched my daddy."

I wondered how long I ought to reckon kin with Luther, but decided to get down to business, slant-wise. "You have something a woman could drink."

The cousin playing with the bass stopped. Hugous shrugged and said, "Woman shouldn't, but a woman could." He fetched a bottle from under the counter and poured me a tiny shot.

It wasn't just liquor. The alcohol wheeled the other chemicals into the bloodstream faster. I felt buzzy and the dust motes seemed to be stars. Deep laugh, then bass chords. I managed to say, "I bet it's a hit."

Hugous nodded. We stared at each other, then I had a vision—Dennis DeSpain riding a still barrel, guiding it through the stars by the coil. Then back to The Door 18. Then a vision: a long pink car with women in it squealing. Then I saw Hugous had moved. "How long does it last?" The ocean swept me away to a steel gull-winged car where an Arab-looking man sat counting money. He looked like the photo Dennis had shown me of his partner.

"Oh, tiny time."

"I was going to ask you if I could sell you some liquor." I waited for another vision, but the special effects seemed to be over.

"No more illegal than untaxed liquor, this stuff. Quick change stuff."

I asked, "Can I have a sample? Maybe I can duplicate it?"

"Sure and a half." Hugous put some in a grapefruit juice bottle. "It been to Tech already, though. Nice, not so much effect you got to have it, mellow, not going to attract lots of attention. Some folks confuse it with having a daydream, like the drug wasn't putting in more than they could do themselves musing."

The alcohol part wasn't missing either. I felt very nice now. "Well, if you need any straight liquor, then I could help you. Where did you get this?"

"Alien up in Franklin County. He cra-zy." Hugous's nephew hit a low bass chord on *crazy* and boinged the strings as though he and Hugous'd rehearsed hitting the emphasis. Or else the drug wasn't completely metabolized out.

"Stupid. Everyone can identify him."

"Maybe he got kin working for him," the nephew said.

Hugous said, not really asking, "Maybe he worse to cross than the law. Uglier than the law."

"Maybe it's like if a dog could take up stilling," I said. "Like he isn't human."

"Or they don't have no idea an alien do the unlawful like us," Hugous's nephew said. I was about to tell him I wasn't an us, when I caught sight of myself in my velveteen dress in the bar mirror.

DeSpain, you turned me into this velveteen fool.

I was starting to move my stuff out to the A-frame when Berenice called me at the dorm. "Marie, what are you doing for the summer?"

Stilling, I thought but didn't say. "I rented a house off in Giles. I have to be out of the dorm by next week."

"I don't want to make this sound like I was looking for a maid, but Lilly's going in to have a hysterectomy. Marie, I don't want to have to go to a nursing home, not even for a month."

If it had been Lilly, I'd have taken offense, but Berenice sounded desperate, which is pitiful in a seventy-six-year-old radical woman. Did I really want to get into stilling? Berenice couldn't wait out my pause and said, "We can help pay next year's tuition."

"I've got a full scholarship."

"Can't you get out of the house in Giles County?"

"Not easy. I'd lose my deposit." And I'd have to move this illegal equipment.

"We can pay for it."

"Let me think about it." Shit, why not? I wouldn't have to distill to pay the summer rent then, or go back to Momma's surrounded by all those various kin, some who wanted me to be starchy like them, the others waiting for me to fall. "Would you want me to clean?"

"No, really, I can manage that. Just help with the groceries, carrying them, not buying them. I've got a power vacuum system in the walls."

"*Je ne suis pas une* maid."

"Of course not. *Vous être* companion. Lilly told me it wasn't cancer. Do you think she's lying? If she still wants me to go to the Institute, then I'm going to be paranoid."

I felt like I'd just tottered back from the edge of a cliff, a criminal career, Dennis DeSpain's black mistress and business partner. "Why would Lilly lie to you about that?" I could keep the house in Giles and sneak off from time to time when Berenice visited old radical friends.

"I just realized she could die before me. It isn't likely, but she could. To spite me. I want her around to rub my feet when I'm dying."

"Oh, Berenice."

"And you'll have to go back to school in the fall."

"Yes, regardless of whatever else happens."

"Good for young people to be tough. You're not headed for the grave, so what concern of yours is it?"

Momma doesn't want me to ever work as a maid, I thought. "I could get paralyzed by a car, and then you and Lilly both would have to take care of me."

Berenice laughed. I might as well have something more legal to do this summer. And Berenice and Lilly would discourage me from going back to DeSpain and making liquor both. I said, "I think you're being a bit fussy, Berenice." My belly was going, *DeSpain, DeSpain*.

"Sorry. Will you help us out?" She sounded much younger then, more like a regular person instead of whizzy Berenice.

"Sure. And you tell me I'm being a fool if I start talking to Dennis DeSpain again."

"Well, we don't want you to do that. Lilly's representing the alien."

"He'll need her soon," I said.

"Explain."

"I shouldn't have said that," I said, remembering their paranoia that their phones were tapped.

"I agree with you, twice," Berenice said.

"I'll bring my stuff over now if you've got a spare room."

"Then it's a done deal." Berenice sounded so relieved. We hung up.

I went downstairs with my computer and saw Dennis waiting by my car. He didn't look angry, so I hoped he hadn't found out about my own still.

"Marie."

"Dennis, I'm going to be taking care of Berenice Nelson while Lilly's in the hospital with surgery."

"Orris thought we were getting too serious. That's when I realized how much I..." Dennis couldn't quite say *wanted*, but he knew *lusted* would be a bit too crude. Seeing him cooled me off, a little. I guess. "Would Berenice...yeah, she'd mind, wouldn't she? How come you're doing maid's work for her?"

"Companion, not maid. Because otherwise, I have to stay at home with all my loser relatives."

"Not all of them are losers, Marie."

"No, but the ones who aren't tell me how stupid it is to have an affair with a cracker bootlegger. No offense, Dennis."

"Orris was threatened because you're at Tech."

"Like if I'd been at New River or cleaning up rooms, Orris would have approved? Jesus, Dennis, how can even a bootlegger stand to be married to such a bitch?"

He twitched his face muscles and froze them. I feared I'd protested too much or that he'd caught some vocal cord corrosion from my breathing in over mash. "Orris made herself into a lady."

Well, I was just insulting his wife. "I'm honored that she considers me a threat, but, Dennis, I quit you. Not the other way around."

"I thought of you when I saw a Chinese Negro Hollins student."

"Go after her then, Dennis."

"She was a whore."

"Dennis, if it takes slutting to get rid of you, I'll take out a license."

"You're not like that."

"Not before I met you, I wasn't. I'm still an honors chemical engineering student. I'm not sleazing around with a poly sci degree just to say I'm not a mill hand."

"You think you're better than us?"

"I will be."

"Christ, Marie. I want to see you again." Then he said, "Lilly's that alien's lawyer, isn't she?" Dennis is so sneaky. Maybe he had my phone tapped to see where I'd be next?

"I don't know."

"When she going in for surgery, Marie?" He started to come closer, but moved back when I stiffened.

"I don't know that, either."

"Well, I can ask around. Probably call her office. Have someone else call. She refused to represent me."

"Well, she has better sense than some people."

"Marie, I just want to talk to you." He ought to have known *talking to* in Black English meant *seeing,* meant *going out with*, all those euphemisms. He smiled slightly as if he'd realized what he'd have said if he'd been talking Black.

"Dennis, what you thinking about that alien?"

"I been seeing sign of its dealing on Loose Trade. And someone got Hugous's account away from me."

"You been following him?"

He shuddered ever so slightly. "I dunno."

I didn't want to provoke Dennis by asking if he feared the alien.

DeSpain Identifies a Trade Rival at Least Once

DeSpain decided the alien seemed to be in the liquor business without anyone's permission—no legal license, even if a man could get one in southwest Virginia, no agreements with the present illegal distributors. But the only thing wrong was that the alien seemed too open about what he was doing. DeSpain sat in front of his computer for an hour as Loose Trade deals popped on and off the screen. He wondered what arcane connections could this alien have.

Orris came in and leaned her breasts against his back. The nipples felt accusing. "How's Steve doing in school?" DeSpain asked.

"I have no idea. You signed his report card last week. I told you I wanted to see it." Her voice rumbled through his body.

"I've got a rival. He hired that Lilly Nelson woman to represent him."

"I've heard that she never represents liquor makers."

"He's that fucking alien. I guess minority something or other played a part, manipulated her sympathies. How is he getting away with it? Who is he paying off?"

"Is he really that much of a threat?"

"Somebody's taken half my nigger accounts."

Orris pulled her breasts out of his back so her voice wasn't vibrating through his spine and ribs but hit him straight in the ears. "You don't need a female black to be helping. What about bringing in a male?"

"I've got to find out what I'm up against." DeSpain sat thinking in front of the keyboard, then exited the system and said, "I'll go pay him a visit. No threats, just sniff around a little."

"Take me out to lunch first."

They drove to The Shogun, where Orris ordered miso soup and a cold noodle dish. DeSpain stared at the octopus legs with their organic suction cups and said, "I'll order in a minute." Orris said, "Europeans think Americans work too much." She and the Japanese chef always slightly mocked every other living being that wasn't Japanese or Orris.

The Japanese chef giggled. DeSpain felt his face turn red. Orris whispered, "Ask him what Japanese eat for lunch."

DeSpain knew what he felt about the businessmen who ordered various sushi cuts set up on plastic slabs, talking about Citicorp, Mitusbishi, and the Orvis catalogue center. "Knowing you, it's miso soup and noodles."

"Precisely."

"Well, bad enough dealing with them all so superior in Tokyo. Now they moving to Roanoke." DeSpain heard the old accent grip his voice and saw the business guys at the table wince. Well, if they were so stupid as to eat sushi for lunch when real Japanese ate miso soup and noodles, DeSpain wasn't going to cringe.

"You couldn't deal with an Osaka bean tractor factory. What makes you think you can cut an alien out of your territory?"

"Shit, Orris. If I'd known you were in this mood, I'd have brung you an Elastrator, and you could snag my balls with the rubber rings."

DeSpain scowled at the business men too dumb to know what to order from a Japanese for lunch.

The chef muttered, "Europeans think Americans work too hard. Europeans must not work at all."

DeSpain said to Orris, "You made his day." He ordered miso soup himself and ate it even if it did seem made from fermented leaves and slightly rotten soy beans. He asked the chef, "Is it hot in Japan?"

"Not all over," the chef said.

When they finished eating, DeSpain said, "Orris, would you want to go with me to see the alien?"

Orris looked as if she wanted to remind him that on their wedding day he'd promised to handle all the illegalities without bothering her. Then she sighed and said, "Why not? If I'm with you, it's just a social call, right."

"Right."

"What about Steve?"

Dennis said, "Go call your Mother and see if she can pick him up at the bus stop."

DeSpain waited. Orris came back from the phone booth and nodded. He helped her in the car and asked, "Scenic route or 220?"

"Let's just get there okay. I don't want to be too late coming home or Mother will worry."

They took 220 to Rocky Mount and picked up 40. Orris said, "I sometimes wish we lived in Roanoke."

"Man once told me Roanoke had the worse vice for a city that size he'd ever seen."

Orris laughed. "I'm not being hypocritical," De-Spain said. "Liquor's not like drugs. People can afford liquor without stealing."

"I said when I married you that I understood what you did. Are you getting too soft, perhaps?"

Shit on Orris when she had these Elastrator moods. They passed out of the rest of Rocky Mount in silence. Then, as they passed Ferrum College and began the mountain part of the ride, Orris said, "I have a tremendous nostalgia for the present."

"What do you mean by that?" DeSpain said, sure that Orris deliberately made a confusing statement.

"Whatever happens at the alien's house will be the future. I love everything in my life up to that moment."

"Even me?"

"I do love you, Dennis. You make my life dramatic, but you're not so brutal that you make me nervous. Even if that reduces your efficiency."

"You think this alien's going to gobble us up."

A semi was laboring up the road, having ignored the warnings back in Woolwine. Orris watched it, Dennis watched it, both wondering if it would collapse on them and make all Orris's fears of the alien moot. It tottered on the turn but didn't fall.

"I saw one once crush a Volkswagen on Route 8," Orris said. "Mother beat me for coming home late. I had to go back and cut across to 58. We'd gone to the beach music festival, and we were going to take the Parkway home."

"You want to go to the beach music festival? It's next week."

"I really am worried about what we're going to be doing in the next hour."

"And you still remember your mamma whipping you for coming home late, even worry about it at twenty-seven-years old. God, Orris, she won't whip Steve because we're late."

"This alien, I hear that he spies on us. He memorizes what people do."

"He knew what I did."

"Did you tell me that?"

"I can't remember."

They shut up again. Dennis looked over at Orris and saw her lips move as if she was worrying them with her teeth, without letting the teeth show. Discreetly scared.

Another truck passed them, on straight enough road that they didn't have to worry. Then Dennis saw a glimpse of faceted ears under a baseball cap, the alien driving a deluxe Oldsmobile van. "That's him," he said to Orris. "In the cruiser van." He found a driveway and turned around.

Orris said, "Maybe the trucks are his, too. It's a bit unusual to see two tractor-trailer rigs trying to make it up Route 40 in the same hour."

"Well, at least he didn't know we were coming," Dennis said, noting the license plate on the cruiser: TURK. It reminded him that he had to fly over to Uralsk the first of July.

The Oldsmobile pulled over. Dennis pulled over behind him. The alien came out of the car and handed Dennis house keys and said, "You can wait for me at my house." His English was better than it had been when DeSpain was fishing on the Smith.

Orris took the alien's house keys from Dennis and said, "Thanks."

Dennis wondered if she'd gone nuts. He asked the alien, "You want us to wait for you at your house. Why?"

"You were looking for me, weren't you?"

"Yes." Dennis wondered for a second how the alien knew, then remembered that he'd turned around to follow the Oldsmobile.

"We should talk, you and I," the alien said. "And you must know where my house is if you were driving this way."

"People gossip," Orris said to the alien as he turned to go back to the Oldsmobile cruiser. The alien shrugged his shoulders before he got back in the car.

DeSpain started his car again. For an instant, he thought about following the alien, now disappearing around a curve. *Those were his trucks. He's really operating at scale.* "What do you think?" he said to Orris.

"It's your business. Is it better to be friendly at first or hostile?"

"I don't know in this case. He's traveling awful conspicuous." He turned toward Patrick County. Orris looked at the alien's house keys. DeSpain glanced over briefly and saw a cylinder key and two computer card keys on the chain.

Yes, those were his trucks, DeSpain thought as they pulled in the dirt road full of double tire tracks just beyond the Patrick County line that would wind back into Franklin. "I know someone's in on this," he said.

"Do you bribe law enforcement officers," Orris asked almost as if it had never occurred to her.

"You're supposed to be discreet." DeSpain tried to sort out the tracks—at least two tractor trailer rigs, the cruiser, and one motorcycle. "This is crazy."

"Unless he has alien weapons." Orris said that as if she'd discarded the thought really, but just wanted to mention it in case.

The Volvo motor cut dead, the car rolling up hill on its own momentum as though the timing belt broke. But it wasn't the kind of car that broke its timing belt. DeSpain threw on the brakes to keep from rolling backward and tried the lights—no electrical system. "You know, if he'd been human," DeSpain said to Orris, "I wouldn't have been so stupid as to take his goddamn keys."

Orris said, "We'll have to wait for him now."

"If he's got a phone, I'm calling a tow truck. Of course, he's got a phone line out."

"Maybe it's dedicated to computers?"

"Orris, I'll get someone to get me a tow truck. I think a motorcycle went in and not out."

Orris sighed and opened the car door. "Shouldn't we push it off the road?"

"Shit." DeSpain saw that he could roll the Volvo backwards downhill. Once he did that, he tried to start it again. It started. Something a few yards away killed electrical systems. He was glad he didn't have a pacemaker. "We can mail him his keys."

Just then, they heard the motorcycle in the distance. Its sound shifted, dopplering in on them. They saw the helmeted motorcyclist dressed in unstudded leathers, a skid scuff along one arm. He stopped, went to a tree, then said, "You can bring the car through now." The voice was broadcast outside the helmet, which was too opaque to see though. The face screen looked newer than the rest of the helmet, which seemed to have been abraded in the same accident that scarred the leather jacket.

DeSpain followed the motorcyclist back to the house, stopping twice when the man got off and fiddled with various trees. The motorcyclist asked, "Do you have the keys? Turk locked me out."

Before DeSpain could decided whether to admit he did, Orris said, "Yes."

The motorcyclist took off his helmet. He had short dark hair and a perfect nose with a matching jawline that DeSpain had priced once at a plastic surgeon's at $25,000. DeSpain wondered what was this clown. He said to the man, "I'm Dennis DeSpain. Turk is the alien, right?" When the man nodded, he kept on, "He sent out a load of liquor."

"We're not sure what to make of this, Mr. DeSpain, but then you're a liquor distributor, too, aren't you?"

"I don't know a man who's proved it in nine years. We've got a hardware store in town, health-food store by the lake, motel, overseas investments."

"Mr. DeSpain, neither the Department of Defense nor the State Department cares about Franklin County illegalities except that an alien is here, modeling his behavior after you people, giving keys to his house to local moonshiners."

"I'm not a moonshiner," DeSpain said. He always associated the terms *moonshine* and *moonshiner* with people from Greensboro who wanted to play folkloristic. "I wanted to meet the alien."

"Why? Don't explain. I know why."

"And why haven't you federal people done anything?"

Orris said, "Why don't we go inside? I'm Orris DeSpain. And what shall we call you?"

"Henry Allen," the man said. Orris gave the keys to DeSpain, who found the hole for the round key and the slots for the two cards. Allen said, "Put the two cards in first, then turn the key. Otherwise, you release the Dobermans."

DeSpain put the cards in carefully, then turned the key. He listened for dogs before he opened the door. "Do you know he's hired a lawyer?"

"We need to know more about Turk and his relationships to the other aliens before we do anything."

"He must know what he'd be doing is illegal, so why don't you bust him?" DeSpain looked around the entranceway and saw nothing alien about it—chrome chandelier, flocked white wallpaper, terrazo tile.

"This way's the living room," Allen said.

They went to the left through an archway. The men sat down on suede chairs, leaving the couch to Orris. She took off one shoe and dragged her nylon-covered toes through the deep pile. DeSpain knew she could feel if the carpet was wool or synthetic, even through her stockings.

"I think he thought I'd go home after we finished talking," Allen said. "So he locked me out. But he knows what I'm doing."

Orris said, "Maybe he has our house bugged? And he didn't want you to meet us."

"Orris," DeSpain said, thinking she'd gone a bit paranoid with that.

"He could easily," Allen said.

"And you letting him bug U.S. citizens?"

"We're trying to see what's going on. We…" The man stopped talking as if realizing that the alien could be listening in now.

A wheeled robot turtle came in and triangulated each of them with its servomotor neck. Allen said, "If you remember anything after it sprays us, call State."

DeSpain only had a vague recollection of it later. He and Orris were driving home when the radio programs told them that five hours had elapsed.

Orris looked at her watch and said, "Mother will be furious."

4

The Game of the Name

I hate it when I can't remember, DeSpain thought as he
shaved himself in the morning. Vague images of a
wheeled turtle named Henry Allen floated through his
mind. He decided he'd gotten drunk with a human co-
hort of the alien's. Nothing had been resolved. The
alien never came back.

Orris watched him from the bathroom door. She
looked haggard without the polish makeup gave her.

"I'm going to see Hugous at The Door 18. He's
buying from the alien."

"Dennis, I think our memories were tampered with.
Maybe you should let this one alone."

"Orris, maybe that alien is just checking out the
territory before whole bunches of alien bootleggers
come in."

"And maybe his kind is going to push us out of the
business. You've got other investments."

"Orris, now you want me to quit." DeSpain wondered if Marie would have dared him on and decided

that she would have. He finished shaving and combed his hair, then put on a suit to show respect to Hugous.

Orris didn't volunteer to come this time. She found the Volvo keys for him and looked down, to the side, as she dangled the keys out to him on her straight-out arm and index finger, as rigid as an admonishing statue.

Be that way, DeSpain thought. Her mother had yelled at them when they picked up Steve, tucking him in the backseat of the Volvo still half asleep.

Hugous was out on a tractor plowing corn land behind The Door 18. DeSpain wondered how, even with income from The Door, the man could afford a balloon-tired air-conditioned cab item like the yellow machine now folding the ends of its giant harrows and turning in the field. The harrows unfolded, and the steel spikes bounced against the clay, then impaled the clods.

DeSpain went through the hanging-open, old hotel door and sat down at the bar, watching the dust motes in the sun coming in through the back window. He figured this'd get some communication from Hugous faster than going out to the field and yelling through the machine noise.

A small camera over the bar swiveled. DeSpain crouched, uneasy. Turtles with mobile, steel necks. He reached over the bar and brought out a bottle and glass. Let's see what the alien's making, he thought. He poured a taste in a glass and drank.

Scuffed leather…call the State Department and ask for Henry Allen…motorcycles…stalled engines.

Damn stuff is drugged. And I was drugged with something the opposite earlier. We didn't get blind drunk.

Hugous came in with just the sweat he'd built up walking away from the air-conditioned tractor cab. He said, "DeSpain. You go on now after you pay me for my liquor."

DeSpain had never heard the man sound so full of menace. He had to call the State Department, ask for Henry Allen before this alien's man did something worse to his memory. "How much I owe you?"

Hugous's chest rumbled something too nasty to be a chuckle. "About five hundred dollars from all the time you cheat me," he said, "but five dollars will cover what you just drank."

DeSpain pulled out a twenty and looked up at the camera. It nodded at him, but then he saw the remote controller in the black man's fist. Hugous nodded, too.

Why doesn't someone stop the alien? What the alien could do to a man's memory was a national security threat. He wasn't just a business rival; he had tricks beyond human nature. DeSpain went to a public phone at a country store on Route 57 near Philpott and used his phone credit card to call the State Department. "I'm looking for a man named Henry Allen," he said to the first human-sounding interactive voice that picked up after the touch-tone connection messages had played.

Another voice, male, replied, "Henry Allen is on vacation."

"I saw him in Franklin County." DeSpain wondered if the alien sent out a bug from The Door 18 to follow him, but continued, "He was observing the alien."

"My information is that he's on vacation. Could you leave a number where he can call you back?"

DeSpain left the number of the motel he co-owned with a third cousin down near the Henry County line, a man who often took messages for him. Then he said, "Look, the alien is selling drugs disguised in bootleg liquor. I think you ought to look into it. He has another drug that destroys more than short-term memory."

"Alcohol does that," the man said.

"It isn't alcohol," DeSpain said. "I seriously advise someone to look into it. Someone else. Henry's too cozy with the alien."

"Mr. DeSpain, our voice-print records show that you served a month of a two-year suspended sentence for liquor distribution when you were nineteen. And your driver's license was suspended. What are you trying to pull?"

"Okay, okay, I used to sell liquor. The alien is doing it now, and he's mixed drugs in it. Memory flash drugs."

"Mr. DeSpain, I advise you to mind your own business."

I am, DeSpain thought. "Henry asked me to call him at the State Department if I got any memories back. I'm doing precisely that now."

"Henry Allen is on vacation."

DeSpain hung up and wondered if Henry Allen would be reprimanded for speaking to a felon. Then he wondered if that bitch Marie knew enough biochemistry to make an antidote to the alien's drugs.

He thought about calling her, remembered how nasty Marie's mother was. Instead, he called up the Virginia Alcohol Beverage Control Board—this is how people at the stills went from being independent to employees of distributors in the first place.

"ABC," the voice answered.

"I'd like to report a still." DeSpain hoped the ABC office didn't have a voice analyzer. "The alien who's living below Ferrum."

"You want to give a name?"

"No."

"Sounds dubious to me. Why should this alien be making liquor?"

"Send one of your people to The Door 18 on Route 666 in Patrick County." DeSpain heard a helicopter flying over, toward the phone booth. He hung up the phone. The helicopter swung around overhead. He pulled out his Beretta and wished he'd thought to bring a gas mask. The gun felt hot in his hand. DeSpain hoped he wasn't being bombarded with microwaves.

The phone rang. *Should I shoot or answer it?*

He picked up the phone and breathed into it, just to let whoever know someone was listening. "DeSpain? This is Henry Allen."

"Are you in the helicopter?"

"I can hear it. I'm sorry, DeSpain."

DeSpain stepped outside, checked the helicopter's belly for police insignia, and raised his gun, fired, missed the gas tanks. The helicopter swung out of range and hovered.

Allen yelled into the phone. DeSpain went to pick up the receiver and said, "Fortunately, the helicopter didn't seem to have an effective drug delivery system on board. So, what can you do for me?"

"I need help evaluating the situation."

"Your alien's drugging the liquor supplies. Is this your helicopter out there? State Department? CIA?"

"Go in the grocery and wait."

DeSpain wondered if the clerks had called the deputies already, but crouched down and ran to the store. A man behind the cash register had a twelve-gauge pointing at DeSpain's belly. DeSpain smiled and tried to put his automatic up. Outside, the helicopter had grappled his car's front bumper and was half dragging, half lifting it away.

"Dennis DeSpain, who are you messing with these days?" the man with the twelve-gauge said.

DeSpain remembered the man now: as a teenager, he'd driven liquor to Roanoke for DeSpain when his daddy was in jail. DeSpain finally got his automatic back in its holster. "Jack, sorry, Jack. I don't know who's out there, but it's not ABC or local law."

"Aliens abducted a couple from around here," one of the other men in the store said. "They used a helicopter just like that." The machine he pointed to had finally winched DeSpain's Volvo under its belly and was flying away.

DeSpain wondered if all the hillbilly paranoia about aliens was accurate, a real war going on while most Americans watched television. The helicopter came back and landed outside the phone booth. The alien, wearing body armor and a helmet, got out and spoke into the phone.

"Son of a bitch," DeSpain said. "I'm going to call the fucking State Department back and tell them they lied."

One of the guys said. "Government always lies. DeSpain, you especially ought to know that."

The alien started toward the store, slowly. Half the guys in the store pulled out boot knives or handguns. A Yankee woman began screaming when the man next to her pulled an Uzi out of his attaché case. DeSpain nodded to the man with the Uzi—Jones, a competitor who occasionally tried to set up shop around the 122 bridge. Jones said to the woman, who'd shut it down to gasping, "You go outside and make peace, you think guns so bad."

The woman was going toward the door when the phone rang. The store manager swung his twelve-gauge around across his shoulder and answered the phone, "Kirtland General Store." He handed the phone to DeSpain and said, "Guy named Allen."

DeSpain said into the phone, "The son of a bitch stole my car, he tinkered with my memory, he's coming in now."

Allen said, "Tell him he needs to talk to Droymaruse."

DeSpain said, "Tell him to talk to Droymaruse? Who the fuck is Droymaruse, and what the fuck good will that do?"

"It's another one of his people," Allen said.

At the same time, the woman said, "I'll give him the message." She was pretty brave for a pacifist, DeSpain thought as she went to the door, opened it, and said, "You need to talk to Droymaruse."

The alien stopped and turned around. DeSpain asked Allen, "What the fuck was that all about?"

"Droymaruse claims he doesn't know what he's doing, either."

The helicopter blades began turning. DeSpain wondered whether he could drive his car away, if he dared. He said to the world at large, "I need a beer."

Allen's voice from the receiver seemed remote. He seemed to be saying, "I'll come pick you up." De-Spain wondered if they'd all been drugged anyway. He couldn't remember feeling this buzzed since the night the ABC and state drug people snagged his car. Almost like the helicopter had done today, but it had been a big road hook adapted from gear used to land planes on carriers. Popped up out of the highway and bang-go. They'd tore his car to large metal shreds looking for cocaine even after they found the liquor.

"Here's your beer. We won't charge you for the army," the manager said. He fitted his shotgun back under the counter, then took DeSpain's money. "You've got to drink it off premises," he said when DeSpain popped the top.

"Oh, give me a fucking break," DeSpain said. The other customers stared him down, so DeSpain decided to go out front anyway. He wrapped the can in a brown paper bag and walked through the parking lot to the weeds near a power line, drained the can in two breaths.

Allen came up on his stupid motorcycle. "I don't think your car is drivable. Can you ride on the back of this?"

DeSpain decided to chance it. "But let me drive," he said, aware of his competition watching from inside.

"You have to wear the helmet then. I don't have a spare." Allen handed the helmet to DeSpain, who grunted as he forced the thing on. Allen's braincase was a tad too little.

DeSpain gunned the engine and felt Allen's fingers tighten around his waist, then tap—*be careful with my machine*. Sumbitch pantywaisted cookie pusher, DeSpain thought, twisting his wrist and stomping on the pedals to get the Honda moving. He headed up toward

Franklin County waiting for the helicopter to pounce, but made it home okay.

Orris and Steve came out when they heard the unfamiliar machine. DeSpain wanted to curse them out for not being more careful, but instead introduced Henry Allen, "Mr. Allen is with the State Department. He's helping figure out the alien."

"Glad to meet you. I'm Orris DeSpain and this is our son, Steve. Would you like to come in."

"Your husband and I need to talk. Thanks."

"Tea or coffee?" Orris asked. "I've got fruit compote or a cheese cake."

"Coffee, that's enough," Allen said.

Orris nodded and went to the kitchen. The men sat down, DeSpain and Henry on the couch. DeSpain looked at his son and said, "You know you're not supposed to go outside if you don't recognize the car."

"Sorry," Stevie said.

"We're going to be in the basement talking after we have our coffee."

"Is this man investigating you? Kids at school say you're a bootlegger."

Allen's lip on one side went back, so fast that if DeSpain wasn't looking at him, he would have missed the expression. Allen said, "We're asking your daddy's advice on how to deal with someone who's making drugged liquor."

Damn, DeSpain thought, you have the dialect almost right, Mr. Diplomatic Corps, except that I never wanted my son to know where half the money comes from. Steve looked at his father and sighed like a little old man. He said, "It's okay, Daddy, the teacher says liquor-making should be legal, without taxes."

DeSpain said, "Steve, we're not talking about me. Why don't you go find your mother?"

"But, Daddy, we've been talking about this in school."

"Go. I'll tell you about moonshine later."

Steve went out, his feet dragging his sock toes under.

Allen said, "I thought a moonshine area would be more rugged."

"Never could grow corn on a 45-degree slope," De-Spain said. "Also, how you going to get enough sugar in. In the old days, we used about a ton a week. Took trains to deliver."

"Now there's not much market for moonshine, I suppose," Allen said, "other than the blind pigs."

"As long the price doubles from federal tax, you gonna have a market for it," DeSpain said. "But I've personally gotten out of it."

Allen looked like he was going to contradict De-Spain, but instead asked, "Do you know the alien has a lawyer on retainer? Lilly Nelson."

DeSpain said, "She'd never take human liquor makers as clients unless they were black and she thought they were innocent."

Orris brought in the coffee. Steve, with a little smile on his face, carried in the cups and saucers. Mr. Allen stood, but DeSpain didn't. Orris served them quietly and then said to Steve, "Let's leave the men alone, sweetheart. Dennis, he was in the hall, listening."

"Daddy's talking to a federal man."

Allen said, "I'm not here to bust moonshiners. I'm here to find out what the alien is doing and why."

"Steve, the alien wrecked my memory Wednesday and then tried to attack me today. He isn't one of us just because he makes liquor."

Orris was smiling as if thinking *since when does a new liquor distributor not have to hack a place for himself?* She said, "Steve, now, or we can't go swimming before the pool closes."

"Oh, goody, a bribe. I want to know what's going on."

DeSpain said, "Don't act like such a jerk in front of company."

"Okay, but we can swim all night at my uncle's."

Orris said, "Those people are a bit rough."

Allen said, "Look, if you don't listen to your parents, I'm going to have to swat you."

"Daddy won't let you."

"Come on, Steve, go with your mother, now. Orris, call back before you leave, okay."

After Orris and Steve had left, Allen said, "Droymaruse will keep Turkemaw busy for a few hours. I don't believe they're all tourists, but that's what they claim. Somebody's got to be crew. At least, Droymaruse."

DeSpain needed to check his bulletin boards. Pending deals from Roanoke to the Urals needed his attention soon. His real business could slump while the government used him to fight the alien. Maybe he could make a deal with the alien himself. Lilly Nelson did. Sentimentality for minorities quite overcame her prejudice against distillers. DeSpain said, "Since Reagan, the feds have been out of the still-busting business. Why are you here?"

"We've got information enough to say the business continues, which did surprise me when I was assigned to Turkemaw, but we're more concerned that his people get a good impression of us."

"Like Americans in Russia who were real rollovers. You know how much I had to be fighting that."

"Yes, we're beginning to understand Turkemaw might be probing us in some way, with plausible deniability by the others. It seems a shame to start interplanetary relations on a paranoid basis, though."

"Knew a paranoid once. He had great ideas if you could put them together. I used him for a while in security," DeSpain said. He remembered how the man didn't work out in the end, rather spectacularly, but DeSpain himself had a good working knowledge of plausible deniability.

"I get your meaning," Allen said. "Maybe there were kidnappings."

"Especially of folks who wander about of a night." DeSpain decided he'd drift dialect toward the folksy, keep Allen slightly to way off guard, depending on how bigoted he was. "Folks coming back from something they shouldn't outta gone to might like to be kidnapped." Nope, that comment was a little too perceptive. "So what do you want to do? I ain't had no experience with stereo-speaker-eared creatures."

"Give it a break, DeSpain. I also know you went to Emory and Henry."

"God, you're smarter than I thought you was. Man, you must have gone to Harvard."

"Princeton."

"Even better."

"We know Turk's lawyer is going for surgery in a few days. She'll be pretty inactive for a month. If he put a lawyer on retainer, he must feel vulnerable in a way we haven't spotted yet."

"He's making illegal liquor. He's drugging people."

"State doesn't get involved in disputes between businessmen, even illegal businessmen. That's Department of Justice."

"I resent you implying that I'm in illegal businesses." DeSpain didn't want any competitors, human or alien, to hear what he needed to say. "Let's go out back. Bring your coffee if you want. Orris has a wonderful garden." Any more talk along these lines needed to be done in the trailer, DeSpain decided. DeSpain swept his trailers for bugs and replaced them ever so often, renovating them enough to pick up some profit. Broken-down trailers cluttered the landscape so badly DeSpain could get all he wanted for the hauling. Allen refilled his coffee cup and followed DeSpain out the back door.

This month's trailer sat on concrete blocks about five feet from the ground. A stack of old mill machinery packing boxes made the stairs. Allen climbed up the boxes to the trailer looking like he would rather have crawled but the coffee cup got in his way; then he carefully put his weight onto the trailer floor. DeSpain watched the State Department man look around at the rubber soundproofing, then explained, "I rehab trailers from time to time. Soundproof so the neighbors don't complain about late-hour drilling and sawing."

"I'd have thought you would have your secure room away from home. Don't most people in your business try to keep the family out of it?"

"Orris would worry if I had a place out." Maybe Allen was a new-style federal revenuer, DeSpain thought, running a fancy variant sting operation with this alien. "So what do you want me to do for you, and how much protection will I get? I take it you don't want him gunned down."

"No. We'll protect you, but not for that." Allen put his coffee cup down. "We want to know why he's making liquor. Just like we want to know why one's breeding fish in Africa."

DeSpain smiled slightly, sure the man came stocked with too many stories of bib-overalled pickup truck drivers with semiautomatics in the gun racks. "How did the alien get his attention focused on me?"

"You threaten to inform on independent still men who won't work for you."

"No, not me personally, but it has been done that way." DeSpain wondered if Bobby had gone to talking. "Look, why don't you tell the other aliens what Turkemaw is doing? And if they don't stop him, then you know who is doing what here."

"We don't know that their motivations are human. We won't know why."

"God, you need better spies. Shit, Turk knows us by name and occupation."

Henry Allen sighed. "I had no idea why he was so curious."

"You got him everyone's name, face, occupations?"

"Just eccentrics."

"How am I eccentric?"

"You're a trout-fishing moonshiner. I thought that was pretty funny. Like a radical lawyer living in Rocky Mount."

"So you set me up for him?" DeSpain wondered if people playing by their human rules would be able to deal with aliens. "How much do you know about them?"

"They have space travel and we don't. They know where we live, and we don't know where they live. State and Defense consider both those things to be critical."

"Maybe we ought to belly crawl to 'um and cut a deal."

"Or get some of them to come here and educate us. Americans and Europeans did that for the Japanese."

"Allen, you've got to be able to tell me more than you're telling me. Yes, the man—alien—is taking over some of the local distillers' accounts, and yes, in the past we'd work over trade competitors in various ways. Mostly psychological, like threatening to turn them in to the law. But it was a decent business. Distillers I know never poisoned their buyers with lead salts. Shit, man, one distiller even tested for poisons."

"I notice you're not saying that was you."

"How do I know Turk isn't working for the feds in a tax grab?"

"I can offer you immunity if you testify against him, should we go that route. We need someone who un-derstands the business and who can get close to him."

"Considering he's drugged my memory out when I had my wife with me coming for a social visit, I don't think he exactly trusts me."

"You can find someone for us."

Bobby would be perfect, DeSpain thought. "I might be able to help you, but it's going to take some looking. I really don't have the connections I used to. Honest."

Henry Allen looked around the trailer, moving his head up and down, not just his eyes. He grinned when he saw DeSpain got his point. Yeah, nobody innocent would have a trailer rigged like this. DeSpain decided to get rid of this trailer and use his alternate secure room until this anti-alien deal had gone down.

.

5

Bobby Considers a Proposition Only a Trifle More Appealing

What DeSpain really wanted to do was to take Orris and the boy to the coast, take a charter out to the Gulf Stream, and kill a marlin. If only he were really rich, out of the mountains, with an accent nobody could trace, he could..."

Do what? He had to tell Bobby to get close to the alien. But that might be dangerous if Bobby was so pissed about being bullied into work that he'd side with the alien.

"Orris, I'm going out."

"When will you be back?" she asked, her hands full of flowers she was arranging in a iron Japanese vase.

"By midnight. I'm taking the truck."

He drove to Bobby's after calling a garage to rescue his Volvo. Suit in a truck sure looks weird, he thought as he looked down at himself.

Bobby and his wife were sitting on the front porch snuggling their children, a little skinny girl against Bobby and the ailing baby boy sprawled in his wife's lap. Bobby said to his wife, "Think you better get the chaps inside." The little girl looked at DeSpain and ran. Bobby's wife lifted the boy against her shoulder and stood up. She looked from Bobby to DeSpain, one hand cupped behind the boy's head.

DeSpain came up the porch steps and opened the door for her. He could barely hear her thank-you.

After she was inside, Bobby said, "So what brings you here, Mr. DeSpain?"

"I'm thinking that if you can help me out a little, then I might be willing to see you set up as an independent."

"You want me to go with your nephews and beat on somebody?"

"Bobby, just find me out some information."

"I'm not real good at being sneaky, Mr. DeSpain."

"Well, if you can do this for me, I'll see to it that you don't have to be devious anymore. Get close to the alien, offer him your liquor."

"That's not all."

"Well, I've got to consider what I want to know after you get close to him." DeSpain needed to know how much the alien intended to expand his operation. Maybe this wasn't a fuss, but if it was, and if the local law wouldn't cooperate at all, he could use Bobby to deliver a bomb.

"Shit, DeSpain, you wouldn't ask much."

"Are you afraid of the alien?"

"Sheriff talked about his helicopter and your car over the radio. Claim was, the alien's grapple brake cut loose and you just happened to be snagged. Dennis, maybe you're picking on something you ought not."

DeSpain's belly tightened, but he thought he was keeping his voice right when he said, "State Department is behind us checking."

Bobby said, "Put that way, I'll call on the space guy."

DeSpain said, "If he isn't in the phone book, then I can arrange for you to leave him email." He got up, not quite sure that Bobby wouldn't side with the alien himself, but if it looked like it was going that way, he'd bring in his cousins again.

Will you really leave me alone if I tell you about the alien?"

"Surely."

"Gonna look bad for you if you can't protect your own."

DeSpain didn't think of Bobby as his own.

When the Lawyer's Away

I asked in the recovery room if my operation was over, asked enough times that about the fifth time I was apologizing for asking. After I got that clear and was upstairs, I didn't feel like talking. Nurses came in offering painkillers. One was so nervous when I refused, I took the shot anyway. Stainless-steel staples ran every quarter inch from just below my navel to a finger span above the pubic bone.

I napped for a while, then woke up to see Marie sitting by my bed. She squirmed with all she had to tell me.

"Am I okay?" I asked. I had an oxygen gizmo poked into both nostrils and an intravenous needle holding my wrist rigid.

"It looked like a big gizzard," she told me, "only round."

"The doctor normally shows the organs only to the family." I've heard that only Southern doctors come out with the organs.

"But what I'm really here about is Bobby. He came by to see Berenice this morning. He's scared. DeSpain…"

"Uh. What about the biopsy?"

"I know you're not feeling quite up to working now, but Bobby wonders what it would take to get a court order to keep DeSpain from bothering him."

"What does DeSpain…" *Why did I come back here to practice,* I thought, *when I could have shared a practice in Charlottesville?* People would have let me recover in peace then. "Was my biopsy okay?"

"I don't know. They'd tell you first."

"Marie, I like you a lot and all but—"

"Well, maybe it can wait for a couple of days. De-Spain wants Bobby to check out the alien for him. Spy for him."

"I should be out in another three days. Tell them all to wait."

"Five days. The day of surgery counts as day zero."

I was too tired to suggest anything. Marie put a piece of ice in my mouth, then more spooning ice into my mouth as if it were oatmeal. I threw up. Marie buzzed in a nurse to take care of the pan.

Argh. I don't know if I recovered faster from the worry or not, but after Marie left, I got up to use the toilet. The nurse rolled the IV with one hand and held me up with the other.

"Have you heard anything about the alien?" I asked.

She shook her head, but with nurses, one never can be sure whether the sign is for *no* or *you're not ready to get involved in that yet, honey.*

I slept after she gave me the pain shot, then woke up about four hours later, not particularly in pain, but really awake when the night nurse came in to take my blood pressure, temperature, and pulse.

"Need anything?" she asked.

I mumbled no and closed my eyes. I'd call my alien client tomorrow and advise him to stop doing anything that could get him arrested until I got better.

In the morning, I watched the IV needle keep coming and coming out of my hand as the nurse pulled. "That's why they taped you so good," she said as she covered the hole. As I reached for the phone to call Turk, I felt a dull ache at my wrist bones from the four-inch needle.

Turk's voice reminded me of how weak I still was. "This is your lawyer, Lilly Nelson. Don't mess with Bobby Vipperman. DeSpain's trying to get him to inform on you, but he doesn't want to do it."

"Thank you for the information," the alien said and hung up. I suddenly remembered the first time I'd seen him, how alien he seemed then. Over the phone, I forgot those stereo-speaker ears.

Humans Getting Together

Bobby ignored me. Bobby was what we call a dumb-ass naive racist, so prevalent in southwest Virginia they made DeSpain look good to me. "Berenice, that alien was right behind me, even when I was going ninety. I

83

heard he knows everything in the county. I don't guess anyone could tell me how he came to know DeSpain wanted me to investigate him."

I asked, "Where were you?"

"I was driving around below Ferrum, thinking about spying on him, Marie. Berenice, maybe I should stand up for my own kind and help DeSpain deal with him."

Berenice said, "I'll get you some tea. Sit with Marie while I set up." Bobby sat off from me on the porch while Berenice made iced tea.

"You been seeing DeSpain, Marie?" he finally asked, raising his chin from where he'd been keeping it tucked.

"I'm not talking to DeSpain anymore," I said, flushing. "I told Lilly that DeSpain asked you to spy on Turk. I felt bad about disturbing her."

"But that Turk thing is her client. And you're keeping house for them." He sounded like that was the one thing about me made sense.

I'm helping a friend, not working as a maid."

"I guess."

"Bobby, whatever all bad you want to say about Dennis, he talked to me like I was just another person."

He looked startled. "I'm just not used to talking to college people I didn't grow up with."

Maybe that was it, not racism at all, I wondered. But then Bobby looked away and tightened his face muscles. Maybe he didn't like to be talked down to by Dennis's ex-mistress, but I wasn't in the mood to credit him with a good motive.

Berenice came out with the iced tea. I went back for glasses and she filled them. Bobby almost said something to me, maybe telling me to help the poor old white lady, but he looked back at Berenice.

"All I ever wanted was to work honest," he said.

"All I ever wanted was to work smart and honest," I said.

"Marie, don't bait him."

Poor bastard looked so grateful at Berenice, I sat back and sipped my iced tea. Bobby said, "She's a bigot toward rednecks." My iced tea flew up my nose.

Berenice said, "You both know that Turk is making illegal liquor and drugs, both. Liquor is one thing, but drugs another."

"And we're all humans together," Bobby said.

"Maybe Dennis is playing Turk's role in the Urals?" Berenice said. "Getting ganged up on by the locals or cheating them. It isn't quite clear."

"What we gonna do now, in this country?"

I said, "Lilly warned Turk that Dennis wants you to get information on him."

Bobby set his glass down and stood up and paced. "Oh, Lordy, why'd she do that."

We women both looked at each other as if we'd realized that lawyer's messages that were sensible to a human might work different on alien brains. Berenice said, "I think maybe I ought to go see the alien."

"Lilly's due back day after tomorrow," I said.

"I'll go see him before then," Berenice said. She still had her driver's license, but I knew Lilly tried to keep her from driving. Said enough retired people clogged the roads.

"You...can you go with her?" Bobby said.

"He's selling liquor at The Door 18, so he might not mind a black woman much," I said.

Berenice said, "I've been rather bored lately, for a woman who used to break bank windows."

"Why'd you do that?" Bobby asked.

"Banks represented imperial powers in the world," Berenice replied, her eyes defocusing as she recalled when she was young, blond, and an absolute stone radical. I had kin like that on Staten Island. We left them there even when Granddad was selling lots on our road to maybe common-law wives. Berenice said, "I've got to call Turk for a convenient time."

I rather hoped we couldn't go until after Lilly got back, but Berenice came back out to the porch before we finished our tea and said, "We can come right over now."

Bobby looked grateful. He finished his tea in two big swallows, then took off out of there.

I didn't feel really well, rather nauseated, but Berenice just grinned and handed me the keys to the old miniature Cadillac.

The car was rigged with electronic gadgets from a cellular phone to a radar detector to an old Toshiba laptop computer, everything absolutely dusty. I slid in and wiped the steering wheel off with the second tissue that popped out of the box. Berenice opened the laptop and pushed its jack into the cigarette lighter hole. "The batteries are dead," she said.

"What about the car batteries?" I asked.

"I've been recharging them every month. Some days I get in and just let it run in neutral. Pretty sad, huh."

"Bad for the air to idle a car," I said. Then I realized she must have driven the car here from the last place she'd been really free, not the old aunt needing a niece to take care of her.

"Had the tires changed last year. The old ones rotted through."

"Maybe we should wait until Lilly gets back?"

"She won't be fit for a deal like this for six weeks. And I'm so old, I won't scare him like a younger human."

So I turned the ignition, hoping that it wouldn't start. *This was worse than being a velveteen fool for a white bootlegger,* I thought as the engine cranked and ran with just a few spits at first. We reversed, then went down the driveway.

"Damn fine car. Small for a Caddy, though," Berenice said. She fished out a cable and seemed to be setting up a cellular phone connection to the laptop. I stopped watching when we drove through Rocky Mount, then looked at the rearview mirror to see if we were being followed. Berenice began pecking keys on the laptop. "Aha," she said, "Turk's having trouble expanding."

"That means he's going to be real testy?"

"The humans don't cooperate with him as much as they did when he first set up operations. I was more concerned with the human behavior than his."

"His we going to be looking at soon."

"Marie, he hasn't killed anyone, even when provoked."

"So far," I said.

"Marie, if you're going to be an old lady about this, I should have left you at home." She typed stiffly. I glanced at her fingers and saw how swollen the knuckles were. She paused in the keying in and said, "I hate being an old lady myself."

"What are you doing?"

"Checking Dennis's business volume," she said. "Bobby gave me some clues. I'm in through an aquarium store that handles illicit Asian arrowanas."

"Don't data hackers have to have fast reflexes?" I asked.

"No. An old lady who's methodical. Patient. Did I ever tell you…no, now's not the time. In another case, there was this German who marched through most of the open data on Tymnet. Methodical, yeah like a Methodist." I wondered if her brain had overloaded. She looked up and rubbed her eyes with her middle fingers, hands flat against her face. "I did think the Legion of Doom was terrible."

"Sorry, but I don't know what you're talking about."

"I was older then than Lilly is now." She hit two keys and pulled out the computer-to-phone cord. "Turk could home in on the signal from the phone."

"But he doesn't kill humans," I said.

"Just mucks with their memory, but age is doing that to me already."

"Not today."

"Adrenaline. I remember everything about protest marches. I even remember how testy you were with Bobby just minutes ago."

I wondered if any of the Vietnamese I knew would think she did them any favors but didn't say more, just followed her directions into Patrick County, then back into Franklin on the dirt road that led to Turk's. When I saw the place, I kinda asked, "An alien in a ranch house?"

"He makes it look real alien," Berenice said.

The alien came out dressed in railroader's overalls, not farmer's: that is, the blue and white pin-striped ones, not the solid denim. No shirt, just naked leather skin. One of my aunts used to tell about a Philadelphia man back in the late seventies who'd come to homestead the hills dressed in such things. Turk made pinstripe overalls look more preposterous than I could imagine they could look, even on a doofus white hippie boy. Then, if you looked again, they looked sinister under that alien head, with only the eyes to look human. I wondered if the faceted ear domes were brittle.

"Hi, Turk," Berenice was saying.

"Ah." He paused, sniffed the air, and finished with "Berenice, my lawyer's aunt. And" —another sniff from the wiggling slots— "the woman who visited The Door 18."

I'd heard he was half-about omniscient, but he wasn't on old people and blacks he hadn't gotten files on. "Yes," I said, not wanting to explain that I was Dennis DeSpain's ex-lover and thanking Hugous for not mentioning my name. I remembered one of my great-grandmothers telling me how we always could use white bigotry, let them think us dumb, and sneak around back of the attitude. "I'm Berenice's nurse, Mary." I'd respond to Mary like it was my real name.

Berenice looked over at me curiously, then grinned. Turk waved a bare arm at us, motioning us in. The leather seemed stretchy, not wrinkled over the joints like human skin. He asked, "Does anyone know you're here?"

"Lilly," Berenice said, "and a couple of people in town." Bare and sterile, the hall smelled of disinfectant, but Turk kept leading us into the kitchen, which smelled of alcohol and fruit. It was crammed full of dehydrators, moldy pots, retorts, scraps of stainless steel;

the counters were cut up and bummed in places. Turk looked at the mess and said, "Nobody comes to visit."

Berenice walked around the room, sniffing almost like Turk, her old nostrils in her long nose wobblingly flexible. She said, "I've come to talk about Bobby."

The alien froze. Then he said, "Can I get you something to drink?"

I shook my head. Berenice said, 'Thank you. Water, no ice." She watched the water come out of the tap. "DeSpain attempted to blackmail Bobby into spying on you. Bobby came to us. He doesn't want to get involved."

"He came to you only after I caught him attempting to invade my property," Turk said.

I wanted to say something, but that might spoil my humble maid act. Berenice said, "Don't do anything. Let Lilly work it out when she's better."

"Bobby and Dennis DeSpain are illegal problems for me to have. Not a lawyer's responsibility. Perhaps Lilly could help me with the State Department, as that is a legal problem I have."

Berenice looked like she wondered if her memory was still hyped. "State Department?"

"A man named Henry Allen."

"What do you want Lilly to do?"

"Get an injunction to stop him. I will take care of my illegal business rivals."

I hated myself for wanting to warn Dennis, but my hindbrain threw me a flash of his little white-bread throat sweating, breath and blood bobbing through it. I'd never been just another one of his black mistresses.

"Don't do anything until Lilly gets back. You might not understand as much of human law and custom as you think."

"The State Department knows I'm making illegal liquors, but it does nothing."

"Human custom," Berenice said, "isn't particularly codified anywhere."

"I have human custom for my liquor," Turk said.

I said, "I think we'd better go."

Berenice suddenly looked old and forgetful again. I was about to ask if she knew where she was when she nodded.

As we drove home, she said, "Damn, sometimes," but didn't say more. Her eyes grew vague and trembled in her head. She opened the laptop, but just looked at it as if she'd known once what it could do.

"Took a lot out of you?"

She sighed.

After we got out of the car back at the house, she said, "I'd like to know more about their customs."

"Berenice, there's only so much you can do."

"I think if one thing happens, I can very well do another."

"What?"

"Marie, sometimes you have to defend your own, but who is my own?"

Sounded to me like the old cranial blood vessels were constricting. We went inside and saw the message light blinking on the answering machine.

It was Bobby. "Berenice, I can't let an old lady deal with all this."

I said, "What the fuck does he mean?"

Berenice said, "I hope he doesn't mean he's going to try to help DeSpain regardless."

The next message was from Lilly. "I called, but you aren't in. Turk called and asked if I could get an injunction against the State Department. He said it should be a civil liberties issue. Do you have any idea of what he's talking about?"

Berenice said, "Marie, wouldn't it be nice to have more tea?" She sounded like she was trying not to be the kind of woman supported all through her teenaged years by my great-aunts. A suggestion this was, not an order.

"I'd kinda prefer limeade myself," I said. "I've got some in the freezer."

Berenice said, "Sounds great to me."

"Aren't you going to call Lilly back?"

She reached for the phone as I went to the kitchen to make limeade. When I got back with the pitcher, she said, "We women are just going to sit. That's what Lilly suggested."

I poured her a glass first. "Berenice, that's best."

"I don't think it's best," she said, but I could see that her ankles were swelling.

"Want me to take off your shoes?"

She grimaced, but when I had her shoes off, she reached down stiffly and massaged her ankles. "Go talk to Dennis."

"I—"

"I don't mean you should offer your body in exchange for Bobby. Tell him to leave the alien alone."

"He wouldn't listen to me. It would hurt his gonads if his wife would put him on the phone."

"Chicks to the front," she said. I realized, after a moment of utter doubt as to her sanity, that the phrase came from radical times before women's lib.

"So far Turk hasn't hurt anyone."

"It doesn't look to me like he tried to leave people unbruised."

6

The Semi-Accidental Mess

Bobby was sweating as he told DeSpain what had happened to him, but DeSpain compared it to losing his Volvo to the alien's helicopter and to Henry Allen's memory lapses. After Bobby wound down, DeSpain said, "You must have done something stupid." Bobby looked guiltier than he should. "Tell him you're defecting from me. Just go right up and join him. Don't just nose around on his roads."

"He knows I'm working for you."

"I suspect he does, Bobby." DeSpain hid his anger, easy to do with such a sap. "How do you think he found out about it?"

"I asked Lilly and Berenice to help me."

"Lilly works for the Turk. You ought not have done that, using women. It's real easy, Bobby." DeSpain wasn't sure he cared now what happened to Bobby. "Just go up to the Turk and tell him you want to work for the most aggressive boss."

"Dennis. Mr. DeSpain."

"When I was twelve, I used to sneak out to where the revenuers lived and run a thing so their trunk lights would drain the batteries. I could fix them without ever touching the engine compartment or opening a car door."

"When I was that age, I was milking cows for Daddy"

"You would have been." DeSpain had brought a piece of rebar he'd filed almost through and patched with black wax. He broke the rebar across his knee.

Bobby said, "The old hippie woman was going to see the Turk. With the maid, you know the one you used to—"

"If an aged student agitator and a nigger bitch can see the Turk, then I don't see why you can't talk to him. I meant for you to do something straightforward, not sneak around his operation sites. Of course that made him suspicious."

Bobby's eyes flew sideways like he just thought of something, a lie or maybe a truth he didn't want to tell. The men sat so still that DeSpain heard Bobby's wife inside talking to her babies. Make the boy feel guilty, DeSpain decided, and he said, "You making it dangerous for Lilly and Berenice, dragging them into it."

Bobby didn't answer, but nodded slightly.

DeSpain said, "Bobby, I'll talk to you next week, then." He stood up and brushed off the back of his suit, then made sure he'd scattered the fake rebar wax crumbs. As he went back to his truck, he thought that he could play this several ways.

When he got back home, Henry Allen had posted him a note on LOOSE TRADE. CONSIDER THAT

THE SIXTEEN-INCH LIMIT ON THE SMITH HAS BEEN CHANGED JUST FOR YOU.

Other Loose Trade subscribers had left electronic giggles. DeSpain wondered for a second if Allen was mocking him, then decided to read the message as a license to kill the Turk.

He wasn't sure he could. Might be that the Turk would kill him, and maybe that was what the government wanted. And he wasn't sure that Allen's message had official standing. What was it about deniability? He almost typed *can't be just for me*, then backed up a few days to see what action there'd been earlier. He noticed a complaint from Luck Aquatics for messages they hadn't made and wondered why the hacker hadn't erased the charges. Some ecology freaks, he decided. Ecology, taxes—got so a man couldn't run an air conditioner without a federal permit.

Then he wondered if the message was from the real Henry Allen or if the Turk was luring him into an ambush. He reached for his phone and called the State Department. "Hi, I'm Dennis DeSpain in Franklin County and I want to talk to Henry Allen. I've talked to him before."

"Please hold." DeSpain waited, then the voice came back. "Mr. DeSpain, Henry Allen says you should proceed with caution. He wishes you well on your fishing trip."

"Is self-defense okay?"

Pause for music. "If it legally passes for self-defense."

"Before, I couldn't even defend myself?"

"I'm not privy to interpretations," the voice said. DeSpain hung up, pulled out his microfiche collection, and began going over old court cases beginning with Sidna Allen's trial in the Hillsboro Courthouse shoot-out. Yeah, DeSpain thought, if I'm understanding all this correctly, before the State Department decided not to protect the Turk, if I'd shot him, even in self-defense with him shooting at me first, I'd have pulled time like old Sidna for killing an officer of the court, even when the officers drew first.

Well, now DeSpain could defend himself against the Turk. He wasn't altogether thrilled.

Lilly's Attempted Convalescence

The doctor read me the biopsy report. Even though they hadn't found cancer in what they cut out, and even though the ovaries looked good for another five years, I ought to keep coming back every year for checkups, and, no they didn't get as high as my gallbladder, so I couldn't know what to expect there.

Berenice looked confused when I told her; not one of her better days, I thought. Marie, who'd brought her, said, "So, Berenice, you won't have to go to the nursing home any time soon."

Berenice smiled brightly and said, "Marie's been real good to me." Marie looked a trifle annoyed.

I sensed something, but didn't feel well enough to get into whatever hassle they'd had between them. I said, "Let's get me home. The hospital got their staples back."

I spent a day recovering in my own bed before I got a call from Turk regarding the State Department man, Henry Allen. I was lying down with a pillow against the incision, the phone on speaker mode. "I want to know if you can do anything to keep Henry Allen from encouraging Dennis DeSpain from trying to kill me."

"Can you prove it?"

"He left a message for DeSpain on Loose Trade, saying that the limit on trout sizes was canceled just for him."

I wondered if I could break my retainer contract due to Turk's being a Loose Trade subscriber. "Turk, you don't know what that trash means."

"DeSpain called the State Department for a clarification."

"Look, as your lawyer, I advise you that distilling liquor, much less adding drugs to it, is illegal. DeSpain keeps a low enough profile that while everyone knows what he does, nobody has ever proved he financed a raided still. And I wouldn't take Dennis as a client unless the court assigned me. Dennis can't sue you; you can't sue the State Department. Really, seriously, whatever you're making, stop."

"I think this is an American Civil Liberties action, restraint of trade."

"It's tax evasion."

"It is the forcing of grain and fruit harvesters to sell decomposable products rather than add value by manipulation and set price by aging."

"Why don't you just…" I was about to tell him to give it away, but that wasn't his point. "Make Dennis an offer. Tell him you'll help him. After all, you think the law, not the business, is wrong,"

"Is that legal advice?"

"No, it isn't legal advice. It's personal advice,"

"DeSpain is hunting me. Can I kill his dogs if they attack me?"

I wondered what was going on here. "Please stay out of trouble for a couple of weeks until I've recovered from the surgery .Or perhaps you'd like to find another lawyer while I'm laid up?" Please.

"Do the human laws governing self-defense apply to me?"

"Turk, I'll get you an opinion on that." I guessed I ought to do that now. "I'll get back to you." I wished I could have told him no, but he could sue me for malpractice if he survived an attack.

Is this interplanetary protocol or just common-wealth rules? I wondered as I dialed Withold's office. "Can I speak to Withold?" I said to the secretary. "I need his opinion on a client's options."

"Commonwealth's attorney Withold Brunner."

"Withold, this is Lilly. I'm that alien Turk's lawyer. I just want to clarify a few things. Is Turk going to be legally treated as a human being under the laws of the commonwealth, or is there some sort of diplomatic immunity I should be aware of? Or how would he be treated if he acted against a human in self-defense?"

"Lilly, legally, he's human, subject to state and federal laws. State wanted us to be tolerant at first, but they've pulled out now. Didn't know you were repre-senting bootleggers now."

"Thanks. I was intrigued by the alienness." I called Turk back and told him that he could defend himself. Never take another client on retainer this side of a cor-poration, I decided.

That afternoon Bobby Vipperman came by. Marie let him in and didn't offer anything to him. I lay on the couch half asleep, the surgery line feeling tense.

"Sorry to bother you, ma'am."

"What do you want, Bobby?"

"Just to talk."

"About what, Bobby."

He sighed like he was about to sing. Some of his people were singers in the poverty-stricken days when people needed aesthetic anesthesia against weather so coldly hostile it froze piss in bedside slop jars. Life then was so mean that boils quickly ran to blood poisoning and killed you at sixty. I took a closer look at him and saw that he'd pulled himself into a posture out of that old culture. That's why I'd thought of high lonesome singing. He was making himself into a little artwork fit for a ballad. I said, "I'm tired, Bobby. Can you stay where DeSpain can't find you for a few days until I can get a body mike for you? If he threatens you again and we've got a record of it—"

"It's all right," he said.

"Bobby, Turk can legally defend himself." God, if DeSpain didn't have him by the balls, I didn't know what was. I'd seen men who went to war or riot, then when war and riot ended, became demolition divers, drag racers, all to prove an image of masculinity women over twenty never were impressed with. I didn't understand this emotionally, no more than men understood women's haute couture combat dressing.

I almost asked Bobby to sing one of the old high lonesome songs to me, but by thirty I'd gone beyond where nostalgia crosses into sentimentality.

And I had to get sleep or I'd bitch out my aunt next stupid thing she remembered about the sixties. "Do as I say, Bobby." The other side of this was animal business, a subalpha sucking up to the dog who beat him.

He didn't answer me, just gave me a look like *what can a man expect from a pacifist liberal pinko woman?* and went on his way.

I began to wonder if I'd feel guilty over what seemed to be about to happen. No, I decided, testosterone rules.

Behind the house, I heard the Cadillac start. "Marie?"

Nobody but me was home. I went into my own bedroom and fell asleep against what I feared was going on. A pillow against my belly pushed my stitches back.

Collected Artifacts

"Marie, don't follow him directly there," Berenice told me. "Take 640 up to the parkway."

I said, "Have you noticed how redneck Lilly gets when she's tired?"

"She spent only seventeen years away, split into bits," Berenice said. "And all the mountain shit—it's like brain fungus. You think you've gotten completely modern when bam, you're listening to a string band play a ballad that you're about to reenact in real life. Is it that way for you and the blues culture sometimes?"

"I fucking hate it."

"Yeah, and I bet you've got at least one lowdown dress. Turn here, go up on the parkway and sneak down."

"You don't sound like a big-city radical woman now."

"Yeah."

"Bobby's hopeless. What are you planning to do, Berenice?"

"I want to see what happens."

I ran up 640 as fast as I could without rounding a curve at fifty-five and smashing some slow old boy. "I'm a chemical engineering student at Tech," I said.

"Meaning," Berenice said, "that all this—and De-Spain, too—is hopelessly out of context?"

I felt like three hundred years of rust was moving in on my stainless-steel lab equipment. "I've got to remember why I hate Hugous and The Door 18."

"Don't have to hate them."

"He's buying liquor from this Turk."

Berenice shut up then. I wondered a second if I wasn't on the wrong side, but drove on. Sometimes sides don't matter as much as being loyal.

No, Tech student, I told myself, that's an attitude that'll yank all your accomplishments right out from under you. "What's important, Berenice, being right or being loyal?"

"Sometimes you don't have the least fucking idea," she said. "I remember cops charging a late-night march on East 79th Street, seeing the fire-mouths, the ones who talked heavy trashing, lose it, seeing the Puerto Rican garage attendants grinning and waving. We cowered among Mercedes and Porsches while the garage guys closed the doors. Odd. We amused them, more than anything else, but those Puerto Ricans save our asses from a beating."

"Meaning?"

"Panic is disgraceful. I remember thinking that I'd rather get clubbed than to panic."

God, she was losing it. I hoped she'd know what she was doing when we got to the Turk's. Was I obeying her because she was a white woman, as dotty as she was? Had the bastards gotten that far into me?

The Turk was waiting for us at the house. He'd folded Bobby over one arm, and his pinstripe overalls were bloody.

I stopped the car. Berenice said, "Reverse slowly."

I looked at her. Her face was immobile, her breathing shallow. Then I began backing. Something stalled the car out, and the Turk came up and draped Bobby across the hood. "Good-bye," he told us. Berenice didn't look at him.

I started the car again, fearing that I'd flooded it. I couldn't look at Bobby laying across the hood, so I backed all the way out into Patrick County.

When we reached hardtop, Berenice and I lifted Bobby's body. It stretched. "He's got no spine," Berenice said. I pulled his shirt aside and saw the incision sewn back up. My heart lurched. *At least the alien has to cut to get at them*, I thought. We lugged Bobby's taffy body into the trunk and drove to call the Franklin County sheriff.

"The alien said it was self-defense," the sheriff said. "He has tapes to prove it, he says."

Faked? An alien who could stall your car out; we'd never know, I thought. We waited by the store for the ambulance.

"Berenice, we should have stopped him."

She shook her head, but I couldn't figure precisely what she meant.

When we got back to Lilly's house, the high wailing time had come. Bobby's wife, Sylvia, had her nails raking her face, screams coming out against Lilly and DeSpain. Her children in the car bawled to see their momma so upset, out of control.

She came at me with "his nigger bitch lover."

Berenice took her hands before she got me. I said, "I didn't put DeSpain up to anything."

"You cunt and a half." She might have been outraged, but not enough to be fighting an old woman. Berenice kept holding Sylvia's hands.

Dennis drove up then with Orris in a new car, a Saab. We nodded to each other and she smiled slightly, like *is he worth it to fight over?* Sylvia turned away from Berenice and screamed at Dennis, "You killed him, you coward bastard."

"I didn't tell him to attack the Turk," Dennis said. "Still, I'll take care of you."

Orris looked at Sylvia, then back at me, then straight ahead over the Saab's sloping hood. She reached over and cut the lights off while Dennis kept talking, "Bobby was a good man. He wanted to defend us against the alien."

"You bastard, you and your overeducated hillbilly wife and your nigger bitch…you killed him."

"Sylvia, I didn't want it to happen this way."

I looked back at Orris. She mouthed something at me. I jerked my head *what* and she said, "You'll find out."

Dennis stopped trying to soothe Sylvia and looked at Orris, who shrugged. She said, "Sylvia, we will take care of you. Why don't you call your minister and go home? Your children are scared to see you like this."

Sylvia looked at her children, who shrank back as if she were a stranger. "Oh, babies, I'm sorry your momma was so nasty-mouthed, but these people killed your daddy."

Berenice said, "I'm so sorry, Sylvia." She hugged Sylvia once, then stepped back. Lilly stared at DeSpain.

"Dennis," I said, "you ought go." And flinched to hear myself drop the infinitive marker *to* in front of Miss Orris.

"He going," Orris said. I didn't know if she was mocking me or dropping from stress into her own first tongue. We looked at each other again. I felt like we women had made a conspiracy against Dennis, but for doing what I wasn't sure.

Lilly said, "Sylvia, I can't drive yet, but I can ride with you to the emergency room. If you don't mind, Marie will take your car and the children back home."

Dennis started his car and was out of there. Sylvia said, "Can she sit with them until I get home?" She hadn't asked me, but I nodded. She looked exhausted now, face soppy with tears, wrinkles etching in heavier, a mill woman married to another mill hand. Half the income now, she'd drop down into welfare unless Dennis did take care of her. Racism was Sylvia's secret defense against knowing where in the social heap she was. I could play maid one night.

"Thanks, Marie," Lilly said, meaning more than Sylvia could understand.

The kids cried on the way home. I bathed them and rocked them. The sickly baby sucked on my arm as if he thought his mother had died and I could be recruited for the role if he tried hard enough.

Lilly and Sylvia pulled up after I got them to sleep. Sylvia looked drugged. Lilly said, "We've arranged for a forensic autopsy anyway. And we've been talking to the funeral home and her minister. "

You're the Turk's lawyer, I thought.

Sylvia said, "Are my babies okay?"

"They're asleep," I said. "Please don't wake them."

"I want to see them."

She went in and put her hand on the boy's chest to see if he still breathed. We led her off to her own bed when she stumbled. "He's been sick," she said as Lilly and I undressed her.

"Do you want either of us to stay?" Lilly asked.

"I'm fine," Sylvia said. "My sister will be over in the morning. She's on third shift."

I wished we'd get out of here—the poverty made me feel guilty for being a college student, for having a schoolteacher mother. We went back to the living room with the framed photos of kin, weddings, and babies. Sylvia put her hands to her face and twitched her head. Lilly and I left.

"I guess she'll be all right," I said. "Dennis can't afford not to take care of her."

Lilly said, "Dennis will for a while. When people forget, he'll quit."

"How are you doing?"

"I'm going to sleep for the next twenty-four hours."

"You shouldn't let people bother you while you're like this."

"I told them to wait, didn't I?"

We drove home. Lilly winced as she got out of the car, bracing her hands against the doorframe. She reached for her surgical scar, but pulled her hands away as if remembering she shouldn't touch it. I helped her

105

with her shower to make sure she didn't fall, then gave her a pain pill and a sleeping pill. "Enough. You've got to get better first."

She pushed a pillow against her belly and said, "Should I let them all kill each other?"

"None of those trash are worth getting sick over. Go to sleep." I pulled the sheet over her.

As Lilly turned to her side and adjusted the pillow against her incision, I looked out her back bedroom window and stopped myself from exclaiming out loud, *Oh, shit.* The old compact Cadillac was gone. *You can't deal with this, Lilly,* I thought as I looked back at her in bed, eyes blinking in the dark, not quite asleep.

I went downstairs to call the sheriff, thinking about Bobby's body folded over his arm. No spine. I wondered if the Turk collected spines as trophies. Well, I thought, maybe Berenice was old enough to die. Old radical like her, she'd probably get a kick out of it and die biting and head-butting, too.

I said to the dispatcher, "Berenice Nelson, Lilly Nelson's aunt, is out driving in a 1986 compact Cadillac. She's too old to be doing this."

"Does she have a valid driver's license?"

"Yes, she has her license but—"

"Has she been declared incompetent?"

"No. How long does she have to be missing before you do anything?"

"Twenty-four hours, unless her mental state was clouded or confused the last time you saw her."

"Well, actually, she threatened to deal with the alien, so doesn't that qualify as confused?"

Don't Take the Spine, That's Alien

DeSpain knew that he had to avenge Bobby's death if he was going to get his black accounts back. He put on the bulletproof vest with the false muscle lines, found the infrared goggles, then called his cousins. His cousins said they were busy, so he drove the truck into Rocky Mount and picked up a couple of guys at Jeb's Old War Parlor. "It'll be a good fight," DeSpain said. "I'll pay you five hundred each."

One man smiled and asked, "Where are your cousins?" But the others weren't listening. Three of them, two logging crew workers with less than twenty fingers between them and a loudmouth fool DeSpain planned to put on point, nodded. They followed DeSpain out and climbed in back of the truck. "Any of you have a bike?" he asked them. Get them in first, he thought, then come in behind and shoot the fucker.

The mouthy one did, a huge overdone Harley. DeSpain said, "That's all right. I've got something lighter back at the house." They detoured back to pick up the moped the law made Dennis use after his liquor-running bust.

That would do. If the motor shorted out, DeSpain could pedal it. He gunned the truck to keep the guys in back from laughing and headed through the night toward the Turk's.

The guys in back yelled at each other and into the wind. DeSpain didn't care what they said. He was rather glad now that he wasn't using cousins. His left foot tapped against the bottom strip around the doorframe, then went to the clutch for the turn off 40. He'd thought about going around on the mountainside, but no, pass the sheep farm, then turn, turn again.

DeSpain stopped the truck. "Here, you take it down to the house," he told the fat mouthy one. "I'll follow right behind you. Road's rough.' If the truck stalls out, then we'll have to walk in."

"We're going after the alien," one of the other men said softly.

"Damn straight," DeSpain said. "He killed Bobby Vipperman. Yanked out his spine."

"Bobby was no fighter," the fat mouthy man said.

Just like you, DeSpain thought, but he said, "Bobby was a bit soft or he'd"—no, can't say *or he'd have got himself out of the mill* because that's probably where kin of theirs worked—"have taken the Turk out."

"I see the Turk in town," the third man said softly. "He knows important people. State Department man was with him."

"The State Department told me the Turk's fair game now." The men DeSpain had hired squeezed in the cab together. The older logger drove. DeSpain started the moped, swearing praise for lithium batteries. If I can't get this alien, he might as well take me, DeSpain thought. He touched his nine-millimeter Beretta in his shoulder holster and the knife against his back. His spine, too sympathetic with Bobby Vipperman's spine, seemed to twist under the knife.

The truck stalled. The fat man got out and, screaming, ran back through the dark. The radio sudden cut on, induced into playing by the strong electric currents. Turk talked alien at them through the radio, obvious, terrible threats.

The two men still in the truck watched as DeSpain's moped stalled out. "Guess we get seven hundred fifty each," the younger logger said, scratching his nose with the stub of his index finger.

"Seems like it," DeSpain said. "You want more beer before we go in?"

"Not hardly," the man said, looking at the other man, who could have been his older brother. "You got two more pair of those night goggles? Are we beating or shooting?"

"Defend yourselves however."

"Maybe we should talk a thousand," the older man said. "Seems like it's a bit more dangerous than poaching black walnut logs."

"Here." DeSpain said, fishing for his wallet, "I'll give you both three hundred each before seven hundred after."

"Write us a note on it," the younger man said.

"The Turk knows we're here. We better get moving," DeSpain said.

"He'll wonder why we're sitting out here," the older man said, "and maybe come out of the house. Write us the note."

DeSpain wrote them a promise for seven hundred each after they talked to the Turk. Away from the house, that was where they ought to confront the alien. He thought, *next time, man or woman, alien or human, gets in my face, I'm going to kill 'em first offense.*

The two loggers let DeSpain pass them. He pedaled the moped up as far as he could go without actually seeing the house, then stopped and pulled down the night goggles. A ghost of infrared behind the trees. Too hot to get a good reading through these cheap goggles.

He yelled, hoping those stereo speaker ears were keen enough to hear him. "Turk, we've got to talk."

"My lawyer's aunt warned me you were coming."

Shit on the old bat. "Don't believe what she told you. She's crazy."

"You and she are not in collaboration." The alien said it like he was reading voice stresses. DeSpain figured maybe stress analyzers came with the ears.

The two loggers stopped. "Come up to the house alone," the Turk called.

DeSpain whispered, "You won't get paid."

The older man said, "We've got enough."

"He'll kill you anyway," DeSpain said. "He can identify you through your voices."

"Don't believe Mr. DeSpain," the alien said.

"Hell, I'm one of you. He's alien. He's selling drugs. I just sell liquor."

"Dennis, this alien stops the truck, he tore out Bobby Vipperman's spine, he's buddies with Hugous at The Door 18, and you want all two of us to march on him?" The men stared at the gun in Dennis's hand.

He looked at it himself, then said, "Do what you want to. You'll have run off and left me."

They did. He thought about shooting them, but went on toward the Turk. Maybe we should work together, he thought, but I don't understand the motivations. Why here? Why liquor? Why with the blacks first? He said, "I'm not coming in your house where you can drug me."

"Fine. We'll come out with lights, action, cameras. I'll even have a human witness."

Berenice, Marie's friend, bitches both. DeSpain sweated under his bulletproof vest. The damn thing seemed glued to him by now, heavier than before, loaded with quarts of sweat. He put the Beretta in his front waistband, pointed to the left. Neither his spine nor his legs wanted him to walk forward, but he could force his body forward by thinking about how everyone would pick him apart if he couldn't deal with this alien. He wondered if news that an alien pushed him off his home territory would get back to Uralsk. The Armenians were being difficult enough as was. Forward, get a look at the guy through the goggles if he's hotter than 75 degrees at the surface.

If he sees infrared, DeSpain realized, he'll know I've got a bulletproof vest on...damn, damn, damn.

"Mr. Dennis DeSpain, who served time for running liquor while drunk," the Turk said, as if identifying Dennis for all time with his previous lowest moment.

"Turk, who the State Department no longer protects," DeSpain said, watching the heat patch resolve into two figures, one Berenice, tiny, uniformly warm across the body, the other the Turk, large, with cold blotches over the head and torso. *I bet I could see him if I took the goggles off.*

"I can't see," Berenice said. "What are you doing?" Bastard's lights flared infrared. DeSpain clawed the goggles away from his eyes, blinded from glare. He threw himself toward the bushes he'd seen before, pulled his gun, and tried to hear sounds, fire at sounds.

But speakers cut on, electric guitars being mutilated by band saws, microphones being run through hammer mills. "Mary and Jesus Chain," he thought someone shouted. A chitinous foot pinned his gun hand. He tried to kick, but the damn thing had such reflexes. The Turk had him by a leg. The foot against his hand

111

squeezed its toes until he dropped the gun. Then the alien lifted DeSpain, still blinded, and tied his legs together. Another heave and he was dangling head down on what had to have been a hook. DeSpain wondered why the alien didn't just hook him through his Achilles tendons. Maybe Bobby's tendons hadn't held?

Then he heard a whuffled gunshot, a crack, and a second shot that went splat. The terrible sound stopped and he was just dangling blind there, wondering if the shots had been inside the electronic equipment or out. After a second DeSpain said, "I can't see."

"Figured you couldn't." It was Berenice. "I couldn't for an instant myself even though I'd closed my eyes. He didn't figure an old lady'd get him. The back of his neck cracked like a lobster."

"You warned him I was coming."

"Shit, Dennis, if I cut you loose, can you fall okay? If it was me up there, I'd break a hip coming down."

"Cut me loose."

"First, the Turk knew you'd come before I even told him. I told him so he'd let me get at his back." DeSpain fell onto the alien's body, which half grabbed at him. He scuttled away and tried to blink away the green blobs still blinding him. Berenice kept talking. "I couldn't know whether I could get through the skull, and I didn't know where he had vital organs, so I went for his neck. One shot to crack him, the second to get the neuroconnectors."

DeSpain said, "Do you know where there's a phone in the house?"

"I'll drive you home. I don't want to explain the gun I used. Plastic. I used to have friends like that, smuggle them onto airplanes."

"I could say Henry Allen gave it to me."

"Dennis, I'll tell everyone you saved me. Let you keep your balls on with the other distributors, and I won't have to explain this gun."

Marie Cleans Up

I got there too late to do anything, passed the alien dead next to a hook with cut ropes. Berenice and Dennis were walking up the steps to front door, both looking tired and sweaty.

"I killed him," Dennis said. "In self-defense." Berenice got the door open; maybe the alien had been so sure of himself that it wasn't locked. We went in the house and saw Bobby's spine, cleaned white, curved like a fish over the mantel. Berenice said, "It looks rather handsome." Dennis shuddered. I thought it jangled between weirdly beautiful and grotesque—conceptual overload and exhaustion running my visual centers like the spine was an optical illusion.

Berenice found the phone and called the sheriff's department. I took the phone from her and told the dispatcher, "You shits couldn't investigate right away, could you?"

When the deputies arrived, they told Berenice to wipe the prints off the gun and help them destroy the tapes that were still rolling out in the yard where Turk had his meat hook. Dennis looked more guilty than I'd ever seen him. "You mean you didn't save her. She saved you?"

"Damn tapes." I loved him then as hard as ever, nakedly happy to be alive, embarrassed for being saved by an old lady.

Onc of the deputies asked, "Where in the hell did she get a plastic pistol?"

The sheriff himself arrived in his business suit and after listening to a few people said to Berenice, "If you weren't as old as you are, we'd arrest you. Marie, take her home." They stripped Dennis of his bulletproof vest and his knife, and cuffed him.

"Take him straight to the hospital and call Dr. Tucker," Berenice said. "The lights blinded him. If you don't take care of him, he'll sue."

She never gets the keys again, I decided as I drove the Cadillac home. Halfway home, Berenice slumped over, asleep and drooling, looking a mess in the early morning sun.

7

Aftermath for the Lawyer

Neither Marie nor Berenice woke me up when they got back. The first I heard about the second killing was at ten-thirty when Orris DeSpain called me to ask about filing separation papers.

"Marie was there again," she said, "and your aunt. Berenice killed Turk while Dennis dangled helpless. They brought out Bobby's spine and took it to the funeral home for burial."

But I'd told them all to wait. "What are you talking about?" I said. Why didn't they let me know what was going on? "Berenice?"

"Berenice. The alien turned his back on her, and she killed him with a plastic explosives gun." Orris sounded as though she'd always known Berenice was dangerous.

I'd ask Marie. Berenice would lie. "Okay, Orris, but why are you filing separation papers?"

"I'm going for a law degree at George Washington University. It makes more sense than shooting Dennis or Marie. What is this, some ballad with me as the villainess against the Nut Brown Maid?"

"Get another lawyer, Orris. I really don't want to hear about it." I figured she'd just called me to see what I'd known about the situation.

I got furious. Then my incision started throbbing, so I just lay back in bed, carefully bent so to relieve tension on that.

Berenice came in then and said, "I think we should tell you that your client Turkemaw is dead."

"Orris DeSpain told me. Damn you, I told all of you to wait."

Berenice sat down in a chair by my bed and looked at her hands, turning them this way and that. "If I'da been younger, I'da been in trouble. What if Turk's people don't understand? I could have been risking the planet."

"Wasn't it self-defense?"

"I killed him to save that Dennis DeSpain. Shit, was Dennis any better? Used the plastic gun. Never knew where that gun came from other than someone stole it. Never knew why I kept it, either."

I said, "Don't forget what he did to Bobby."

She said, "I'm confused about Bobby. Isn't he dead?"

Two days later, when I was trying to sleep in the afternoon, still using a pillow to hold the stitches in, a couple more aliens and a State Department man came by.

The other aliens were more alien than Turk. How, I wasn't sure, but as soon as I saw the other aliens, I knew Turk had been pushing his own limits the way he pushed Dennis DeSpain's. He hadn't been born or bred to be human, but he was crazy enough to fake it. These new aliens wore sashes and wristbands, not blue coveralls, and looked neater than Turk had looked. And they didn't look a bit like tourists.

"Was there a reason to kill Turkemaw?" the State Department guy asked. He wasn't the one I'd seen with Turk earlier.

Berenice said, "I'm sorry, but he was killing humans."

One of the aliens said, "We wondered," so flatly I decided they had rather globally wondered and sent us Turk to see how we'd react. A test. These aliens would never explain how the test worked. No right way, no wrong way, no blame.

"Is Dennis free then?" I asked.

"Your local law is holding him for the gun he couldn't use." The alien sounded vaguely confused, but then nobody arrested Berenice for her much-more-illegal gun, that CIA special that someone, probably a European leftist studying war in the Middle East, had stolen thirty years earlier, a talisman gun that had drifted around radical circles until Berenice stopped it when she returned to Rocky Mount.

The State Department man asked Berenice, "Do you remember who gave you that gun?"

"An old lady my age remember something like that?" Her eyes went vague, unfocused, then flickered toward me. Yes, I thought, absolutely, but nobody pushed for an answer. Both the State Department guy and the aliens stood for a few seconds looking at Berenice as though she were a monument, then left without saying good-bye.

After the door closed, Berenice said, "I'm sorry all this came at the time it did. I feel most guilty that I did enjoy it. Just a little, you understand. I hadn't been out like that in a long damn time."

I wished I wasn't getting the impression she'd done the right thing. And I pitied Turk, even if he were the alien equivalent of Dennis DeSpain. Someone trickier than he let him come. "Just don't get into more trouble until mid-August." I decided I'd have to take care of Bobby's kids—I'd been half responsible for him getting killed.

"I didn't mean to get you upset. And I didn't save Bobby, did I? All I got out of it was some more memories." She stopped as if checking that at least those memories moved from short-term to long-term memory. "I didn't think I could get more memories at my age. But poor Bobby."

Neither of us saved Bobby, old aunt. The warranty on my body has expired, even if the biopsy was negative, and here we are, later in life than we imagined when we were younger. In your radical days, did you ever expect to be so old? I thought I'd skip middle age myself, but no.

Yes, I was glad she showed Rocky Mount a bit of the old young Berenice who'd run radical in the streets.

Orris filed her separation papers with commonwealth's attorney Withold Brunner representing her. Everyone thought that bitchy of her, but she didn't betray any of Dennis's illegal business. But then Dennis rolled over when he heard who her lawyer was.

As Orris said she was going to do, she went to Georgetown University, but instead of returning to Rocky Mount or Roanoke as a lawyer, she became a State Department officer. When she was back once, trolling for gossip about Dennis and Marie, she said, "Henry Allen inspired me to do it?

"He seemed rather doofus to me," I said.

"Precisely. I knew I could do a better job."

Some time in the next year I sold the miniature Cadillac to make sure Berenice never again went adventuring and came home after signing the papers to incredible guilt. With the sale of her car or the death she'd caused or just aging in general, she never again was as clear or vigorous as the night she killed the alien. Sylvia, Bobby's widow, helped me with her. I felt odd, no possible children of my own, but with a sudden family that I had to support. I began taking bootleggers as clients.

Marie had married Dennis when the divorce was final. He told all his buddies he did it to strengthen his alliances with his black dealers. Rumor in the rougher bars and jukes had it Berenice had been about to shoot him next when Marie saved him. My bootlegger clients kept me informed as to various twists of the county's oral traditions.

When Marie got her chemical engineering degree a few years later, she applied for a legal distilling license for fuel-grade alcohol. They hired me to help them. We took it out in Marie's name because of Dennis's record.

Dennis saved Marie from becoming the officious techie I had imagined as her future when I first met her. Her white husband seemed to have made her wicked enough to be tolerant of human foibles—Berenice's senility, her outlaw cousins. With DeSpain with her, even trout fishing probably seemed erotic and slimy fun dirty. Whatever, years after Marie got her chemical engineering degree and her legal liquor license, you could suspect she still kept a shake-baby dress or two. I hoped she didn't think keeping a space for her outlaw side was a failing. I saw it as a sign of grace.

But poor Dennis. By the time he was forty, he was strictly legal.

We all met around Berenice's grave sometime after he'd turned forty-three. Marie wore a light purple velveteen dress that I knew wasn't disrespectful of the mourners of this particular dead.

Marie said, "Berenice said this color would make a white woman look yellow green. She said I ought to wear it a lot."

I said, "She refused to believe that you'd turn out to be just another dye-house chemist."

Marie looked at Dennis and said, "Is it so different?"

Dennis said, "We're doing better than that, Marie." He seemed embarrassed. He said, "Lilly, I'm sorry."

I knew he meant for Bobby, and just nodded. But then don't we middle-class Southerners always fail the rednecks who trust us? When Bobby was in high school, he asked his daddy's supervisor about getting in a support group for the college-bound. The supervisor earlier had said to the social worker organizing the group, "You damn fool, you're stealing my best future workers." And the supervisor told Bobby he'd be happier avoiding high-class anxieties and the college-bound support group was just a scam to give the social worker a job.

Funny, how I'd forgotten that until now.

The aliens neither invaded nor gave us FTL drive diagrams. Not while I was alive, at least.

Last time we heard about Orris, she was the American cultural attaché to Angola. *Time* magazine printed a photo of her driving a Land-Rover out of the embassy gates with the president's daughter. She was laughing.

Biography

Rebecca Ore was born in Louisville, KY, out of people from Kentucky and Virginia, Irish Catholic and French Protestant turned Southern Baptist on her mother's side and Welsh and Borderer on her father's. She grew up in South Carolina and fell in love with New York City from a distance, moved there in 1968 and lived on the Upper West Side and Lower East Side for seven years. Somehow, she also attended Columbia University School of General Studies while spending most of her energy in the St. Mark's Poetry Project. In 1975, she moved to San Francisco for almost a year, then moved to Virginia, back and forth several places for several years, finished a Masters in English, then moved to rural Virginia for ten years, writing sf novels and living in her grandparent's house after they died. She's now owner of a small house in Philadelphia with a walled garden, one wall stone and brick, one wall stone against a hill, and the west wall not there as the neighbor and she share the space.

She owns a Border Terrier named Kit and grows roses and hostas. She's currently an academic gypsy and has been variously an editorial assistant for the Science Fiction Book Club, a reporter/photographer for the Patrick County *Enterprise*, and a assistant landscape gardener.